MORLOCK NIGHT

"Fun, strange and slightly disturbing."
Paul Magrs

"One of the three foundational Steampunk texts."
Retrospeculation

"Jeter is an exhilarating writer who always seems to have another rabbit to pull out of his hat."
The New York Times Book Review

"Jeter has a few good cards to play. The vision of a Morlock-devastated world is suitably horrifying. Best of all is the lore of the London sewers (where else would Morlocks set up shop?), thick with fascinating details lifted from Mayhew's *London Labour & London Poor* – giving a feel of authenticity unattainable by the more traditional auctorial study of Wells, Doyle and the rest. An entertaining romp."
Foundation

"K. W. Jeter [is] one of the most audacious and wildly inventive science fiction writers currently putting pen to paper."
Ontario Journal

K W JETER

Morlock Night

With an Introduction by Tim Powers
& an Afterword from Adam Roberts

ANGRY
ROBOT

ANGRY ROBOT
An imprint of Watkins Media Ltd

Lace Market House,
54-56 High Pavement,
Nottingham,
NG1 1HW
UK

angryrobotbooks.com
twitter.com/angryrobotbooks
Back to the future

Originally published in 1979
This Angry Robot edition 2011

Cover by John Coulthart
Set in Meridien by THL Design

Distributed in the United States by Penguin Random House, Inc., New York.

ISBN 978 0 85766 100 5
Ebook ISBN 978 0 85766 101 2

Printed in the United States of America

9 8 7 6 5 4 3

To Dorothea Kenney

INTRODUCTION
By Tim Powers

It was K. W. Jeter who, in the letter column of the April 1987 issue of *Locus* magazine, coined the word "Steampunk" to describe some books he and James Blaylock and I were writing at the time. Cyberpunk was the literary movement current in science fiction then, so Jeter jokingly proposed the new term for our stuff, "based on the appropriate technology of the era".

When I searched for the word on Google this evening, the search engine (almost a Steampunk term right there) returned well over six million results. And though there were precursors, books by Ronald Clark and Michael Moorcock and Harry Harrison, it was Jeter's *Morlock Night* in 1979 that really started it all – all the books and movies about extraordinary gentlemen in capes and top hats scurrying through foggy night-time London on secret errands that involve infernal devices and wonderful machines with elaborate scrollwork on the gears and levers.

I believe it was early in 1976 that Roger Elwood told K. W. Jeter, Ray Nelson and I that a British publisher wanted a series of ten books based on the idea of King Arthur being reincarnated throughout the centuries, obligingly reappearing whenever England needed rescuing. The three of us agreed to write them, and we got together to divvy up history, being sure to leave enough years between adventures for Arthur to have time to be born and grow to adulthood. As I recall, we kind of haggled over various dates, but Jeter came away with the clear claim on Victorian England. I'm glad now that Nelson and I missed grabbing that slot – neither of us could have written anything like *Morlock Night*.

The deal with the British publisher fell apart, but *Morlock Night* found an American publisher, and then a different British one, and readers on both sides of the Atlantic got to experience Jeter's unique Victorian London.

And it is unique. I think Blaylock might have visited England before he wrote books like *Homunculus*, but neither Jeter nor I had any first-hand knowledge of the place. Nevertheless,

Blaylock, Jeter and I spent many afternoons over endless pitchers of beer in a bar called O'Hara's, hatching extravagant science fiction and fantasy plots set in London as we variously imagined it.

Jeter discovered the priceless source book, Henry Mayhew's *London Labour and London Poor*, and Blaylock and I made eager use of it too. And when I recently asked Jeter about other sources, he said, "Anything else I probably swiped from reading Victorian novelists, including William Harrison Ainsworth, who was probably the best, or at least the most lurid, of the Victorian 'pulp' novelists, not that that term was used to describe writers like him back then; right at the moment I'm re-reading his GUY FAWKES [...] and enjoying it a great deal; quite a reminder of just how damn good were even the Victorian writers who are now considered minor or completely forgotten. Or just flat-out maligned, such as Bulwer-Lytton, who was frankly a great writer, and any snotty little college professor who disagrees can kiss my ass; feel free to quote me in that exact language. George Gissing is considered to have been a fairly serious writer, and I read quite a few of his novels, particularly his early ones, such as *Demos* and *The Nether World*, which are much more grimly Dickensian in tone than his later ones."

In other words, Jeter had a fully realized London in his head, and if it didn't conform precisely to the actual London of 1895, it derived from richly enhanced contemporary models. The result, *Morlock Night*, is a book that almost reads as if H. Rider Haggard had written it, rather than a young 20th century Californian.

Almost. Jeter's book bangs along at a much faster pace than Haggard's books did, and the deadpan humor is all Jeter's. The "excitable and unrestrained" character of the Morlocks as they angrily try to work a machine hopelessly beyond their comprehension is wonderful to see, and the impatient banter between Edwin Hocker and Tafe is entertainingly discordant – just by the phrasing of Tafe's comments, we soon catch on that she's from a more modern time.

Not that it's all beer and skittles, by any means. There are perils, and they're downright apocalyptic. The doom that threatens the world – "Nothing comes after this […] And nothing before, either […] My dear fellow […] this is no *end* to everything, this *is* everything" – is a nightmare vision right out of Philip K. Dick.

But Jeter's London is, as well as dangerous,

endlessly colorful and grotesque – the underground Lost Coin World, with the vast corroded-together conglomeration of swords and coins and antediluvian submarines known as the Grand Tosh – the Edinburgh scholar whose pursuit of Atlantean artifacts has led him to retire forever into the London sewers – the malevolent mummy in the castle of Montsegur–!

Without knowing that he was breaking a new trail that would one day be a conduit for lots of books and movies and graphic novels and clothing and jewelry and God knows what all, Jeter in this book pointed out a new and fascinating direction… and then even provided the enduring name for it.

I'm glad the book that started it all is back in print for a new generation of readers.

Tim Powers, January 2011

MORLOCK NIGHT

"... *and another – a quiet, shy man with a beard – whom I didn't know, and who, as far as my observation went, never opened his mouth all the evening.*"

H. G. Wells, *The Time Machine*

I
Mr Hocker Begins

"An astonishing narrative, don't you think?"

"What? Oh... yes. Yes, indeed. Quite incredible." In truth, I hadn't even been aware of the other's presence at my side until he spoke. Darkness and fog had all but swallowed up the landmarks of the city so familiar to me. The prideful namesake of the Lion Brewery had glared down at me as I passed, then was gone; I had thought myself all alone as I walked through the thickening London night air, beneath the gas lamps flaring a sulphurous yellow through the mist. Now my private universe was halved by this quiet-stepping other.

"Incredible?" he echoed and allowed his fine lips to trace the barest motion of a smile. "Perhaps. Perhaps."

Now that I had directed my attention toward him, I was amused that so striking a figure could have paced anywhere near the corner of my eye without forcing himself to the centre of my thoughts. Swathed in an overcoat so black it seemed a hole into which the dim street light poured and was swallowed up – indeed, my companion appeared to be an animated fragment of the night itself, with the glossy points of his patent boots the only stars. And the face! A pale moon to be sure! Handsome enough with dark eyes and sensuous mouth beneath lustrous jet hair, but a complexion of such a pallor that I couldn't help wondering what illness or unnatural habits had blanched him thus.

"So you find his story beyond belief, eh?" asked the Pale Man – for so I had already begun to identify him in my own mind – as we paced farther down the street.

My opinion escaped in a contemptuous snort. "If our host really expected us to believe his outlandish tale," said I, "then he badly misjudged his audience, I'm afraid. A Machine for Travelling through Time! Whizzing along through millions of years to find our descendants divided into cannibalistic brutes

below the ground and effete wastrels above!
What rot. A very pretty bedtime fable for the
pessimistic, atheistic, and socialistic, but… no
more than that, I'm sure."

"Eh! And is that all–" The Pale Man
whipped a slender ebony walking stick from
his far side and blocked my progress with it.
"Is that all his story signified to you?"

I brushed the stick away from my chest and
resumed my walk. My unwanted companion's
singular rudeness stiffened the tenor of my
voice as I replied, "A cracking good evening's
entertainment I thought it, which, supplied
with a more uplifting ending, would make a diverting fiction for The Strand. If I find time to
put it down on paper I shall certainly submit it
to the editors of that periodical. And now, sir–"

"Oh, don't bother trying to write it," interrupted the Pale Man. "One of our host's
other guests will do a perfectly adequate job
of recording it, in about – let's see – this is
1892, isn't it?"

"For God's sake, man," I said in exasperation, "of course it is! How befuddled are you?"
Had I a drunkard beside me?

"Yes," mused the Pale Man, touching his
chin with his black gloved hand, "in about

three years time I see Mr. Wells writing it. Yes, 1895 would be the date. That is, of course, if there ever is an 1895."

"And why shouldn't there be?" A drunkard, and an apocalyptist to boot! On the spot I resolved to set foot no more in a parlour that attracted such queer ducks. The private income left to me by my late father enabled me to pursue my diversions as I wished – principally the study of the ancient Celtic language and artefacts – but in leading such a fetterless life I did receive the damnedest invitations. Dinners where the host babbled about his Time Machine! But no more. Better my usual solitude than any more such nonsense.

"Ah, yes. There will always be an England, won't there?"

My companion had a most irritating half-smile, as though prompted by the smug contemplation of someone else's stupidity. "And a solid, happy world for it to sit upon like a green and prosperous jewel. Eh? That's the way it looks to you now, doesn't it?"

"And to anyone else with eyes to see." I decided to cut short what further arguments I now anticipated from him. "Sir, the like of your sentiments has been echoed by scores of crazed loons teetering on soap crates in every public park in London – all to sway the course of English empire no more than summer breezes do upon Gibraltar! I care not for the exact label you place on your foolishness, be it anarchism, socialism, land reform, Owenism, or whatever. To me it is muddle-headedness at best, damnable knavery at worst. And now, sir, I will be taking my leave of–"

"Not yet," he rudely commanded. With a vice-like grip he laid hold of my arm. "You mistake me. Petty politics concern me not at all." He let go and the blood throbbed back into my arm.

I sighed and resigned myself to further conversation. Doubtless this person meant to accompany me all the way to my front door. And farther than that? No, if necessary, a boot would keep him out of my own parlour – a satisfying thought. Since my youth I had worked out daily with a set of Indian clubs and had done a little boxing at school, so despite my slender physique I had little fear of a tussle with this boorish fellow.

"And what does interest you then?" I asked. I found my crusted old briar in my coat pocket and brought it to my mouth, as I meant to place a smoker's defensive veil between him and myself. But further probing and thumping of my pockets didn't turn up my tobacco pouch; an annoyance, as I felt sure I had had it when I had left my host for the evening's residence.

"Here. Try some of mine." My pallid companion extended toward me a black Morocco envelope. "Help yourself, Mr. Hocker. It is Mr. Edwin Hocker, isn't it?"

"Yes, of course it is," I murmured as I looked into his pouch. It was filled with a crude shag of almost sinister darkness, perfect velvet with tiny oily glints. Still, a pipe can't be taken out of one's mouth without having been lit – at least satisfactorily, that is. I filled mine and lit it from my box of safety matches. The shag turned out to be nowhere as harsh as its forbidding appearance had suggested. Soon a dense nimbus of smoke was added to the thick fog pressing in around us.

The Pale Man put his pouch away without filling a pipe of his own."

"I'm interested in evil," he said abruptly. "And blood and death."

"Their propagation or suppression?" I asked in amusement.

"Do not make light of such things," he whispered ominously, and glared at me with such intensity that my teeth froze upon the stem of my briar. "What seems most secure and solid to you rests in fact on a ground eaten away from below. This comfortable world of yours is poised above an abyss of such darkness and despair as to make the story you heard a little while ago seem like nothing but the overture whose themes but foreshadow the awful climaxes of Death's, worst opera!"

His bloodless visage and sudden passion of voice raised the hackles on my neck and the keenest apprehension. in my breast. Mad? Deranged? What in Hell was I smoking, anyway? My head felt dizzy from the smoke. Was I being drugged? I decided to throwaway the whole pipe if I detected any opiate effect from his suspicious, if pleasant smoking, gift. For the moment I tried to allay my fears by glancing surreptitiously around me for the best route of escape, in case my companion became violent. I was willing to take on a drunkard, but not a lunatic. The fog had grown even denser, obscuring all but the closest street lamps. I felt sure I'd be able to lose him in it, if need be.

"Ah… hmmm. Yes," I managed to say beneath his vehement stare. "Death, you say?"

His former sardonic humour seemed to filter back into his face. "Don't be alarmed. At least… not yet. Let us just speculate for the time being." His gaze turned away from me and into the dark fog where our steps were leading. "Let us suppose the story we heard tonight is true. And that our host did build a Time Machine, on the saddle of which he travelled into the far distant future, and then back here again."

"An easy enough supposition," I said between puffs on my briar, "if one's not called upon to believe it."

The Pale Man ignored me and went on. "Let us also suppose that he travels to the future again, as he says he intends, to that distant epoch he told us so much of. Only this time the clever ones, the Morlocks–"

"Beastly coinage!" I interjected. "What an imagination the man has!"

"–as I say, the Morlocks, but the really clever ones instead of the mere workers and foot-soldiers he grappled with; the Morlock generals, let's say! These are waiting for him the next time, they direct the ambush that overpowers our host – and our host's bones are tossed into an open grave millions of years removed from the day of his birth!" The disturbing vehemence had returned to his voice.

"My good fellow, don't get so excited over a mere story! Divert yourself with whatever sequels you care to imagine, but save such passion for reality."

"Eh? What about that?" he said in a frenzy. "What if it all happens – or is to happen – that way?"

"*If* it all happens thus," I answered wearily, "it would well serve the damned fool for meddling around with such outlandish notions. Time Machine, indeed!"

"You miss the true import of such an occurrence. All men die – don't they? – and our late host will be no more homeless a few million years from now than he would be if he were planted in his own garden. Dirt is eternal. But what of the Machine? Eh? What of *it*?"

I fanned a little of the thick tobacco fumes away from my face. "I imagine that our hypothetical Morlocks would take their supposed Time Machine and scoot up and down the duration of God's own creation with the bloody thing."

The Pale Man held up his gloved hand. "A little more speculation, if you please. Let us say our, ahem, supposed Morlocks have acquired the Machine as we say, but they don't use it to travel all over Time. No, they find instead they can only travel with it to one point in Time – our own. What then?"

"Yes, well, I suspect they'd come to see us. Like day excursions across the Channel. Be introduced to Queen Victoria at the court, like wild Indians were before Elizabeth." It struck me that we had been walking for quite some time. Where was my house? We must have passed it or made a wrong turning in the fog without my knowing, and thus entered some section of the city unknown to me. A factory district? Through the uncommonly dense mist I could see no glimmer of street lamps, but only a few dull red glares, like foundry fires. But burning at this late hour? Surely a constable would soon come into view, who could direct me properly.

But for the moment I dreaded the thought

of being abandoned in the swirling, impene-
trable fog more than I had previously
abhorred my strange companion. His pallid
face, the outlines of which I could still make
out beside me despite the gloom, was even
welcome now. Still, I kept an eye out for my
longed-for constable.

"Day excursions?" said the Pale Man. "At
first perhaps, but then... Can you not think
of another time, long ago when rude eyes
measured the breadth of this land from a distance, and hearts foreign to ours longed to
own its green fields?"

"You speak very handsomely," I allowed.
"But a proper love for Queen and country
shouldn't drive you to excessive fancies. Get
hold of yourself, man. It was an evening's
dubious entertainment, but nothing more
than that. And even if these imaginary Morlocks were hot with greed and poised on the
lip of our world like the Visigoths eyeing
Rome, what could you – or I – do about it?
It took a hero such as King Arthur to drive
out the invaders in the Fifth Century. It
would take another hero such as he to fight
off the fiends that our host's and your imagination have conjured up! And where, pray,

could such an Arthur Redivivus be found?! I knew I was taking a risk in going along with a possible lunacy, but I hoped that my companion's obsession might be purged by forcing it to some sort of logical conclusion. Then our conversation could be turned to more constructive channels such as finding our way out of the unknown lane into which we had wandered.

"Arthur Redivivus, eh?" His features, even in the dark and mist, sharpened with excitement. "By God, you are the man I wanted!"

I restrained myself from asking if he often had difficulty in finding people to listen to his nonsense. "I say – do you recognise the area we're in? This damned fog–"

"Never mind that," he snapped. "Keep your mind on the important things."

"My dear sir. I am damp, tired, and my feet are beginning to hurt from this endless perambulation. Nothing strikes me as more pressing than the immediate relief of all three conditions."

"Damn your petty mind," the Pale Man said with some heat. "Cavities of blood and horror yawn beneath your steps, and all you worry about is the condition of your shoe leather."

Clearly there was to be no getting around the fellow's monomania, and my patience was exhausted. "Good night," I said determinedly. "Our paths separate here. I am for home and bed – wherever they are – and you are free to seek out some other poor soul upon whom you may vent your ravings. Time Machines! Morlocks! King Arthur, indeed! *Bosh*, is all!" I turned on my heel and stalked away from him.

"Find your way home, then!" I heard him call after me, with the sardonic humour that had been brewing all along breaking at last into cruel laughter. "You'll have another conversation with Doctor Ambrose after you've learned a few things!"

In Hell, I thought angrily. I turned around to make some cutting retort, but his form had already vanished into the dark night and fog. Suddenly, the taste of his tobacco burning in my briar became cloying upon my tongue. The fumes clotted sickeningly. I pulled the pipe from my mouth and dashed it to the ground. From the bowl the burning shag spilled, hissing and spitting with a dull red glow like the larger fires I could see through the mist. I ground the loathsome

cinders under my boot, then – my heart filling with a sudden, unreasoning fear –
hurried blindly away from the spot and into
the darkness that swelled around me.

2
The London Battleground

Damnable fool, I thought as I strode on. Did I mean my odd companion of late or myself? No matter. Anger, as it will, had replaced fear. A whole evening behind me wasted on such nonsense, and now I had a few more hours to look forward to of floundering about in the clammy fog before I found myself in my own warm home. Without bearings I pressed on, cursing myself and all the other doltards the English race produces.

Mercifully the fog began to thin and lift. Soon I could see the stars' pinpoints of light through rifts in the scudding clouds overhead. A three-quarters moon broke through and further illuminated the scene. My relief at being able to see around me, though, was soon chased away by a growing dismay.

The section of London in which I found myself was completely unrecognisable to me. Indeed, I was appalled to discover that such an area even existed. Were our municipal authorities really so lax as to allow it? I saw now that the buildings beside which I had been walking were actually nothing but ru- ined shells, great walls of brick and stone shattered into jag-topped pieces surrounded by mounds of rubble. Twisted pipes and charred, broken timbers poked out of the de- bris like skeletal fingers. What horrendous disaster could have struck this quarter and left me so unaware of its having happened?

And when could it have happened? Even now I could see that tangled clumps of weeds had burst forth in the crevices of the rubble. The whole area, as far as my eye could detect in any direction, gave the im- pression of violent destruction, overlaid with years of abandonment and neglect. For thirty years, as child and man, I had lived in London and never been aware that its boundaries contained such a monumental landscape of collapse.

Had I wandered so far in the fog as to have entered an area somehow forgotten by nearly everyone in the city? For a moment I feared that the images of ruin were all disordered hallucinations brought upon me by the sinister tobacco – if that's what it really was – of Dr. Ambrose – if that was his true name. But then I was confronted with a shoulder-high isthmus of broken stone that spilled across the road. No other route lay before me; I was forced to scramble and pick my way over it. The sharp edges of the stones against my palms convinced me of the reality of my surroundings. Wherever this was I had strayed to, it was as undeniable as the tear in the knee of my trousers inflicted by one of the shards.

On the other side of the rubble's barricade I could discern more clearly the distant fires I had first glimpsed through the fog. I had mistakenly thought them to be small and nearby – the contained, productive furnaces of factory work. Instead, I saw now that the nearest was some miles away and engulfed. a large, multi-storied building. Even as I watched, one of the outer walls cracked from the heat and fell away, revealing the pulsing white heart of the conflagration. Columns of turgid smoke billowed upwards, uniting in the sky with the dark outpourings from the further blazes.

My God, I thought, appalled. Some calamity had broken loose upon one of the inner sections – of the city as I had wandered about. For a moment my legs nearly trembled out from under me and I fell back against the sloping rubble I had just crossed. In fear and awe I gaped at the scene ahead of me. It seemed as though I was gazing into one of the fiery circles of Hell itself. In my breast bloomed the desire to creep into some dust-lined pit of broken masonry and hide myself from the sight of the flames. I suppressed the shameful fear as well as I could and regained my feet. Hampered by darkness and the street's mounded litter, I hurried toward the burning buildings – both to render what assistance I could and to regain my bearings in the city.

Before I had gone more than a few hundred yards I found the ruined nature of the district I was in assuming the aspect of some forgotten battlefield. Raw-edged craters pocked the street's surface, with curved segments of ruptured water and sewer conduits glinting dully from pools of stagnant water. I threaded my way cautiously among the pits, fearing the misstep that the dim moonlight made likely.

The shattered walls of the buildings along the sides of the road had become more grotesque in their appearance, reduced even closer to their elementary fragments. With my brain reeling and my heart oppressed by the sights that surrounded me, I pressed on and caught at last in my nostrils the smell of burning that was spreading through the night air like a disease.

Soon I could taste the ashes in my mouth. A subtler, more noisome odour was intermixed with the burning wood and singed brick. A smell such as burning pork might give. Noises – dull, muffled explosions and a sharper, rattling sound like rapid drumbeats – came to my ears from the direction of the flames. These grew louder as I hurried through the devastated landscape.

My mind was so filled with dire conjectures of what calamity had struck this section of London – earthquake, insurrection, God only knew – that I failed to see the rim of the largest crater until my boot crumbled its edge. I fell and slid partway down its rough slope. At the same time I saw three bright scarlet lines cut the darkness over my head, and from behind heard a stuttering crack of rapid gunfire.

An irrational wave of temper swept over me and I raised my head over the rim of the crater. "I say," I shouted at my unseen marksman. "Are you aware you're shooting at a British citizen?" The half-destroyed walls echoed with my words, but gave no answer. "I demand to know—"

I suddenly felt myself grasped about the legs and pulled down farther into the crater, tearing my waistcoat against the rough stones. "What the hell are you doing?" demanded a hoarse woman's voice. At the same time the air above the crater was suddenly crossed and re-crossed with scores of the glaring red trails, while a clattering volley of gunfire sounded from all sides and chips of masonry danced off the walls along the street.

Safe below the hail of shots, I twisted around on the pit's slope and confronted this new personage. I saw a young woman of slight build with close-cropped dark hair. Her fine-boned features were obscured beneath streaks of black grease on her forehead and cheeks. Dressed in a man's rough trousers and jacket, with a belted leather harness crossing her shoulders and waist, she crouched in front of me, cradling some odd type of rifle across her knees.

What this woman and her strange garb signified, I had no idea. By this time so many disorienting events had battered my mind that I felt nothing further could surprise me. "My dear woman," I said, raising my voice. "I find this incredible. We're surrounded by maniacs with some type of Maxim gun up there. What in God's name is going on?"

She stared at me, her eyes drawing into slits. "Something wrong with you, buddy?" she demanded. "And where'd you scavenge those funny clothes?"

"I— I don't know what's wrong." I said weakly, taken aback by a voice so belligerent in a woman – the most shocking thing so far. "I feel a little dizzy. And these were good tweeds before all this madness started."

The gunfire ceased and the crater's interior lapsed into darkness. She turned toward the sky. "We'd better move out," she said. "Before they start flinging in grenades."

"Grenades?" *My God*, I thought. *A war has broken outright in the heart of London*. I fancied myself well up in the news of the day, but I had heard of no diplomatic crisis that could have precipitated this. Had the Kaiser or Czar gone mad and ordered their secret agents – of which London was full, everyone knew – to instigate some wave of assassination and bombing? *Filthy brutes*, I seethed to myself. *Whoever they are. Bringing their infernal devices into the heart of a civilised nation's capital instead of out among some peasants and savages where they belonged.*

"Come on," said the woman. "Lost your gun? Here, take this." She unsnapped a leather holster on her belt and extended a dully gleaming shape of metal to me. I took it and felt the grip of some unfamiliar make of pistol fill my hand. Automatically, my fingers curled around it.

I am no soldier and must confess that, up to this point, my acquaintance with a battlefield had been limited to reading war correspondents' dispatches. But here, in London, to see the ugly face of destruction… I felt as outraged at this violation of the proper order as an astronomer would upon seeing the planets break from their orbits and dance into the sun. I confess that my blood pulsed with a giddy excitement at the chance of placing a bullet into the hearts of whatever scoundrels had invaded – without even proper notification of intent – my homeland's green and sacred soil. God and queen must love a patriot, and there's no patriot like a man with a gun in his hand. I put away whatever qualms I had about the situation in which I had found myself. Whoever this indelicately garbed woman was, I had no choice but to follow her crouching figure to the bottom of the crater.

My tweeds were even worse soiled by the time I had half slid, half-stumbled down. My boots splashed into several inches of muddy, scum-topped water. "Over here," whispered the woman. The dark outline of her hand motioned me to follow. I glanced nervously up at the rim of the crater, saw nothing but the stars and moon overhead, then went along behind her.

I watched as she knelt down and pried up a large broken section of cement, then assisted her in sliding it a few feet away. A jagged hole, slightly wider than a man's shoulders, was revealed now, broken through into some form of tunnel beneath. I surmised it to be a sewer conduit, as a dampish, corrupted smell wafted from the aperture. I looked at it dubiously as the woman slung her rifle behind her by its strap. "Come on, jack," she said. "In you go."

The hole's repugnant aspect held me at its rim, but then we both whirled around at hearing slight scuttling noises behind and above us. My first flush of courage had been tempered by caution. I stowed the strange pistol in my coat pocket and lowered myself feet first into the hole.

A drop of a few feet landed me in a shallow rivulet of water. I stepped back and looked up through the hole, waiting for my female comrade to drop through. Her heavy booted feet and rough-clothed lower limbs appeared, then she descended no farther. Her body twisted violently around. At the hole's perimeter I could see another figure, obscured by darkness, lunge at her from somewhere above.

Their combined weight crumbled away the rim of the hole, and the woman fell another few inches, dragging her assailant partway down with her. I grabbed her feet in order to help pull her through, but to no avail. She was held fast by the figure grappling with her. One arm freed itself and groped blindly behind her for her rifle, but it was wedged hopelessly between her and the edge of the hole. I could see her other hand pushing against one of the assailant's fists, in which a long, bayonet-like blade struck off the moon's light as it strained toward her neck.

Her boots broke from my grasp and kicked against my chest. "What the hell are you waiting for?" she shouted. "Get him!"

I brought the pistol out of my pocket, knelt, and with a hand and eye steady from many grouse shoots, aimed at the narrow section of her attacker that was open to me. Nothing happened when I pulled the gun's trigger. "Come on! Come on, dammit!" she gasped as I fumbled in the sewer's darkness for the pistol's safety release. A tiny lever on its side moved under my thumb and I brought the pistol back up to fire.

As my finger pulled back on the trigger, the woman, instead of keeping her head away from the attacker's blade, lowered it and pushed desperately with her brow against the other's fist. I could make out every tense ligament of her face now filling my line of fire. Too late to stop the shot, I jerked the pistol up as it fired.

The flash from the weapon's muzzle dazzled my eyes, and the sewer tunnel echoed deafeningly with its roar. I peered upward, dreading to see which of them had intercepted my shot.

The woman's body slumped lower, then fell to the tunnel's sloping floor. The other figure slid through as well, landing heavily in the shallow water and not moving as the woman raised herself to her hands and knees.

"Are you all right?" I asked.

She nodded as she slowly regained her breath. By the scrap of light from the hole in the sewer's arching roof, I watched as she stood and unfastened a short tubular object from her belt. A click, and a flaring beam of light shot from one end of it. A peculiar sort of lamp I thought it, but undeniably useful.

I stepped close behind her as she went up to the corpse of her assailant and played the beam of light over it. The skin of my arms and neck contracted in horror as the body's details were revealed by the bright circle travelling over it. My mind raced back to the memory of a fantastic story of a Time Machine and the adventures it produced, told in a warm, well-lit parlour only a few hours – it seemed ages! – ago. My eccentric host's very words leapt into my thoughts… *this bleached, obscene, nocturnal thing… it was a dull white, and had strange, large greyish-red eyes… flaxen hair on its head and down its back…* I shivered involuntarily when I realised that the corpse on the sewer floor before me was the very image of my story-telling host's imaginary Morlocks! Indeed, as I stared at the dead thing, its large eyes still glaring at us, the word imaginary shrank from my thoughts. I stood aghast, bereft of sense as would be an Alpine traveller, who, upon the lifting of a snowstorm, finds himself poised on the very brink of a bottomless precipice.

As we examined the creature's vile carcass, I noted a few significant differences from those details that the Time Machine's inventor had described to his dinner party. Our host had given his audience the impression of a much smaller creature with a thin-shanked, spidery appearance. The one before us now was of the stature of a short man built wide across the shoulders, with corded muscles filling out its sinewy arms. The flaxen hair was clipped short, and the creature was garbed in a one-piece, utilitarian garment, crossed with leather straps like my companion's, but stained with blood from the fatal wound my shot had given him. A rifle similar to the woman's lay under the corpse, while the bayonet was only a few inches from the creature's outflung hand.

My study of this apparition was ended when the woman doused the light. The beam disappeared with only a slight click from the tube she held. "A scout," she said. "We'd better move on before the rest of his squad comes after."

I helped her drag the pallid corpse away from where it would have been visible from above. Then, into the complete darkness and stale must of the sewer tunnel, I followed after her. As I slogged through the shallow water, my mind flicked from thought to thought like the beam of light my companion produced to light our way.

The remembered words of the mysterious Dr. Ambrose taunted me. Clearly he had not been the babbling lunatic I had surmised him to be. A figure of knowledge and power I saw him now; but what knowledge? What power? By his agency, I was certain, I had been translated from my quiet London haunts into this dark vista of struggle and death. A fragment from Matthew Arnold... *as on a darkling plain! Swept with confused alarms of struggle and flight,/Where ignorant armies clash by night* – crossed my thoughts. But what did it signify? Was all this some covert invasion that had erupted in the midst of England of which Ambrose had some advance knowledge? Was there a connection between his pallor and the much ghastlier whiteness of the Morlock I had slain? Could this Ambrose perhaps be an agent of the Morlocks disguised as a man of this time, and drawing me into some devious plot? For what purpose?

Such was the anxious tenor of the musings that absorbed me as I tramped through the damp sewer tunnel. I longed to ply the woman ahead of me with questions – she certainly didn't seem to wonder at these proceedings – but refrained. Simple survival dictated my silence for the moment. Dreadful conjectures of war and disaster sweeping over English soil filled my breast.

I felt one of the woman's hands reach back and push against my chest. "Hold up a second," she whispered, then stepped away from me. The stream of sewage water splashed against my boots as I waited. "All right," she said after a few seconds. "Climb up here."

The beam of her odd lamp illuminated the mouth of another tunnel a few feet above the floor of the one in which I stood. She reached a hand down from her perch and helped me clamber up beside her. "I think this will take us somewhere along the Thames," she said. "We'd better rest for a few minutes before we go up there."

I sat down and leaned my back against the tunnel's curved wall. The long march through the sewer's heavy, oxygen-depleted air had in fact nearly exhausted me. A cool draft of fresh air came from somewhere beyond, though, and we sat in our clammy niche, refreshing our lungs.

"Whose squad you with?" asked my companion at last. I couldn't place the accent in which she formed her terse words.

"Ah… no squad," I said. "Don't have one, you see." I had resolved to conceal my ignorance from her concerning the circumstances into which I had been thrust. To ask point-blank the questions pressing in my brain would most likely convince the woman that I was insane. But if I hid my lack of knowledge about the war raging over our heads, I could perhaps add to my store of facts without exposing myself.

"Freebooting it, huh?" she said. "That's a hard way to go. Though I suppose that's what I've got coming now. Those damned lockers came down on my squad like a ton of bricks. I doubt anyone besides myself got away with his skin on." She lapsed into silence, staring into the lightless depths of the sewer.

"Where are you headed now?" I asked.

"Squeezer's company was pretty well dug into the East End. If we can get past the locker lines and link up with them we'll be doing all right. We can probably get what we need – some food, water and ammo – from Squeezer and his bunch. He owes me a favour."

I mulled over these scraps of information, trying to glean as many inferences as possible from them. Was the word lockers somehow derived from Morlocks? I decided to fish for more information. "Ahh... where will this Squeezer and his men pull back to if the, uh, lockers take the East End?" I assumed the person in question to be some sort of military leader.

"Pull back?" Her face turned toward me. "There isn't any place to pull back to. The East End is it. When that goes, it's all, over."

"Surely," I protested, "there must be somewhere else–"

"There was a radio transmission from Birmingham yesterday. But none today. And the locker bombers were spotted flying that way this morning. The whole city's probably smoking rubble by now." Her voice droned out the chilling statements, the rage and horror suppressed by the need to keep control of one's self.

I didn't ask her what radio transmissions or locker-bombers were.

"But Europe," I said. "Or America. Surely there must be some place that can, help us–"

"What help could a bunch of corpses give us? They were all wiped out months ago." She leaped closer to me. "Are you all right? You didn't get hit in the head or anything, did you?"

"No… no, I'm all right. I just… got confused. That's all. Fatigue, you know." My mind raced giddily at these revelations. *This is the end of it all?* I wondered sickly. Surely the force that had overwhelmed all the rest of the world would have little trouble snuffing out a last ragged band of holdouts in London's East End. And after that?

The dead Morlock's pallid visage and staring red eyes swam before my mind's eye. So inheriting the Earth millions of years hence wasn't enough for the filthy breed! They must swarm all over Time itself until every second of Creation was under their brute heel! And what of Man – the progenitor of these obscene parodies of himself? Subjugated, perhaps, if any survived. Kept as cattle like the far future's Eloi to feed the Morlocks' hideous appetites.

Not my flesh, I vowed silently. A shudder of revulsion and anger swept over me. When London fell I'd take to the countryside, cutting a red path through the Morlocks – with my bare hands when my bullets ran out – until my back was to the edge of the Dover cliffs. The Channel would receive my dying body and wash my ungnawed bones to sea.

I had always thought myself to be a man of moderate passions, indistinguishable in that respect from most Englishmen born to our logical and mannered times. But now my blood was aboil with fierce and dramatic thoughts, inviolate vows and burning vengeances. And I do not think myself uncommon in reacting so. I can imagine but few of my contemporaries reacting with anything but the same emotions of repugnance and defiance as I experienced upon the thought of the Morlocks' invasion. Thus do times of crisis arouse the most vivid, if not always the best, instincts.

"Come on," said my companion, rising to her feet. She started up the tunnel's gentle slope and I followed after, stooping slightly because of the tunnel's smaller diameter. "By the way," she called over her shoulder. "I'm known as Tafe."

"I'm pleased to make your acquaintance," said I. "Edwin Hocker's my name." Thus introduced, we proceeded upwards, away from the sanctuary of the sewer's quiet and dark.

Nothing that had happened so far had prepared me for the sight I witnessed upon reaching the surface of London again. I crawled out of the sewer opening, following Tafe, my new found Amazonian – in temperament if not stature – comrade, and entered a universe whose last vestiges of Order had fallen to brute Chaos.

Through a grate of twisted iron bars we
hoisted ourselves out onto the Albert Em-
bankment. All around us the marks of recent
combat were visible – the rubble of shattered
buildings, the cratered streets, the thick pall
of smoke stinging our eyes. The Embank-
ment's lamp-posts knocked on their sides
like tenpins, with their iron dolphins in the
street's dirt and muck like so many beached
fish gasping for air.

From this point, upriver on the Surrey
side, we could see the fires at London's
heart, billowing out their columns of smoke
that all but obscured the moon and stars.
Massive rumbling noises, like the Earth in
upheaval, together with explosions muffled
by distance, battered our ears from all points
of the compass.

"Let's go," said Tafe. She unslung her rifle
from her back and held it poised before her.

Mute with dismay at the sight of London
in flames, I followed after. The next few
hours melted free of Time and its passing,
merging into an endless nightmare of flight
and the pitiable aspects of a ruined city.

We picked our way across the Thames on
toe twisted remains of some massive bridge

that lay collapsed in the dark water. We scrambled from crater to crater, from mound of rubble to broken wall, tacking a devious course to the East End. Where the passage was impossible due to fire or the presence of the "lockers" as Tafe called them, we back-tracked and went around, or waited until it was clear. Once we crouched in a trench filled with freezing mud while a yard away from us a company of the enemy sauntered past, laughing and gabbling to each other in their barbaric tongue. I lifted my head and caught sight of their pallid, large-eyed faces, filled with a cruel triumph. Then Tafe hissed and pulled me back out of sight.

Visions of death and destruction. Christopher Wren's great church dome shattered. A wide boulevard littered with human corpses plundered of their weapons. Massive metal constructs, bristling with cannon and apparently at one time propelled by wheels inside belts of iron, now butted against each other in frozen combat and leaking greasy smoke from their hatches. Traces of a yellowish gas clinging to the lowest points of a street, at the first sickly-sweet scent of which Tafe turned and ran while I coughed and stumbled after.

Thus we made our way across the city – scrambling, hiding, running – with Tafe leading in her cautious semi-crouch, rifle poised, and I following, dazed by the wreckage.

I came out of my sinking stupor once while we were taking momentary refuge in a gutted cathedral. The great bells had fallen when the supporting timbers had burned away, and now lay on the sides in the charred pews and altar. One side of the chapel, I discovered, had been converted by the Morlocks into a temporary butcher shop for their ravaging troops. In the dark the vague outlines could be seen of the half-stripped carcasses hanging from hooks in this grisly abattoir, swaying and turning over scattered ribcages and spines. I found myself staring at a kettle of rendered fat and suppressing a scream. Suddenly the church itself began to scream, then tilted and went darker than the dark that had filled it before…

Tafe slapped me back into consciousness. The nightmare wasn't over yet. She pulled me to my feet, then led me into the now-empty street outside.

The East End was silent when we at last sneaked into that section of the city, but the pall of smoke and signs of recent battle were clearly evident. We saw none of the Morlocks. They had apparently finished their business and moved on to some other area to celebrate their victory.

We found the remains of Squeezer's company still crouched in the trenches they had dug in the centre of one narrow crossroads. Tafe searched among the still bodies, then stopped and turned over the corpse of an older male, his grey beard. stiff with the mud in which he had fallen. For a moment Tafe laid her ear against the old man's chest, then lowered the cold body back to the ground.

Cold, disheartened, my clothes torn and covered with filth, I stood next to her and shivered as I surveyed the desolate scene around us. The moon was lower now, sliding beneath the smoke that filled the sky. When dawn came, where would we be?

Tafe stood and pointed across the series of trenches. "See if the lockers left any ammo behind. We'll need all we can get our hands on."

We separated and began our unpleasant task, searching around and under the slaughtered forms of men and women, who had been the last flickering light of human society in the besieged city and the world beyond. How many other random sparks like Tafe and myself existed, seeking only to make our own deaths come hard as possible to the Morlocks?

Such was the upshot of one man's ambition to Travel through Time! A man in whose very parlour I had supped at the beginning of this long, dark night, and now whose very memory I cursed in my heart! A Time Machine that had become a bridge for these monsters, our children, to swarm across from millions of years into the future and overwhelm us. In the silenced, blood-spattered face of every brave man I examined was the same question that I read in my own heart. What evil design of Providence could have thus doubled Creation upon itself, like a snake devouring its own tail?

I reached the end of the trench without finding anything more than empty shell casings and a few broken knives. The Morlocks were evidently efficient scavengers of Man and his artefacts. I lowered the final corpse back down to the muddy floor of the trench, straightened my aching back, then leapt back in horror as the corpse in front of me jerked convulsively, flinging its limbs out like a ghastly marionette. A spatter of half-clotted blood struck my face. The corpse sagged back to the ground. Only then did my befogged brain perceive the ringing echo of a gunshot from somewhere close by.

Another shot rang out and the trench's rim exploded into pieces of mud and paving stone a few inches from my head. "Hocker!" I heard Tafe call out. "Get down!" A second of frozen bafflement passed; then I dove full-length to the bottom of the trench. A volley of shots splattered into the wall in front of which I had been standing.

I crawled a few yards away on my stomach, then turned on my side and pulled from my coat the pistol Tafe had given me. All was silent but for my heart's pounding. The shots must have come from one of the ruined buildings that flanked the street. Another lone Morlock? I counted my breaths for a minute, then cautiously raised my head over the trench's rim. The jagged brick walls on either side revealed nothing. At the other end of the trench I could see Tafe crouched with her rifle, scanning the dark, unmoving shapes that surrounded us.

Another minute passed. I began inching my way closer to Tafe, watching the ruins as I pulled myself along on my hands and knees. My ear caught the sound of something moving in the rubble behind a segment of wall several yards away. A few shards of brick were dislodged and pattered to the ground. My hand with the pistol flew up instinctively and I fired twice at the shape I thought I detected in the ruined building.

Nothing moved for several seconds. Was this the end of our lone antagonist or had he merely fled to fetch more of his vile brethren? I was about to raise my head to see when a small object flew in an arc from behind the wall. It bounced off the side of the trench behind me, then rolled a few feet away. A small, oval object, the size of two fists perhaps, with a cross-hatched metal casing, lying in the mud.

Tafe grabbed me roughly by the shoulder and threw me to one side of the trench. Stunned for the moment, I saw her leap upon the grenade, rise to her feet, and throw it into the air back at the ruin from where it had come. It only travelled a few yards from her hand when it exploded.

A glaring flash of light, and a dull percussive sound drove into my head and abdomen. Mud and dirt rained upon me, dislodged from the trench wall by the shrapnel, but where Tafe had thrown me I was safe from the metal shards' actual impact.

She, however, had still been standing with one arm raised when the grenade went off. Now she lay crumpled on the floor of the trench, blood streaming from wounds across her head and neck.

I crawled to her and examined her injuries as well as I could. She was unconscious but breathing. My head jerked up at the sound of movements in the buildings surrounding us. More than one – the other Morlocks had no doubt been attracted by the explosion. The rustling and scraping of their footsteps spread to either side as they fanned out.

Hastily, I tore out most of the lining from my coat, wadded it and pressed it to the largest of Tafe's wounds just below the jaw. With one hand holding the bandage tight, I managed to lift her with my other arm. The heels of her boots made two grooves in the trench's mud as I dragged her from the spot.

At the farthest end of the trench I stopped and listened for the Morlocks. The sound of cautious footsteps in mud led me to surmise that they had come out of the ruins and were starting to filter into the trenches to look for us. The buildings on this side of the crossroads were silent. I scrambled up out of the trench, pulling Tafe with me. As I started to carry her into the nearest battered shell of bricks, rifle fire burst behind us and the mud flew into a gritty spray a few inches from my feet. The next shots hit against the half-destroyed wall I dragged Tafe behind.

The slow, deliberate footsteps from the trenches edged closer toward the small cul-de-sac where I crouched with Tafe's unconscious form against me. Both her rifle and my pistol had been lost in the trench when the grenade had exploded. Her smaller wounds had crusted over with dried blood and dirt, but the rag I held to her neck still seeped red. My own blood felt hot and feverish, pulsing at my temples.

I looked at my own filthy hand, the blood upon it glistening wet in the fragment of moonlight that slid into the ruins, and

waited for the Morlocks to fall upon us.
Noise from beyond the shattered bricks. The
blood and dirt.

3

Cigars and Good Beer

"Come on, Hocker. Wake up. It's not as bad as all that."

The toe of a boot rudely prodded me in the ribs. I opened my eyes, which I thought had closed upon my last earthly vision, and saw Dr. Ambrose standing over me. A thin smile was upon his death-pale, handsome face.

"You!" I cried, raising myself upon my elbows. "Fiend! What ungodly tricks have you been playing upon me?" I would have stood up and taken the man's neck in my hands but for the silver point of his walking stick that he held against my chest.

"Control yourself, Hocker." The smile vanished. "Tricks, indeed! If a blindfolded man was walking upon the edge of a cliff and someone else tore the cloth from his eyes, no matter how much seeing his danger scared the fellow, would you call it a 'trick'? Good Lord, Hocker, you should be grateful to me, instead of spitting out your spleen at me as though you were someone with an actual grievance. Now come on, stand up and pull yourself together, man. All shall be explained. Here, take a swig of this. It'll help clear your head."

He put aside his walking stick, bent down and grasped me by the arm. As he drew me up my legs were a trifle unsteady from muscle fatigue; he pressed a small silver flask to my lips. I drank and found myself swallowing brandy, good but with an unfamiliar aftertaste to it. Its warmth spread across my chest and oddly up the back of my head. My dizziness and a ringing in my ears melted away and my tired legs stopped trembling.

Ambrose took away the nearly empty flask and stowed it in his coat "Got your heart back again?" he asked.

I nodded, then looked at the scene around us. Another wave of dismay swept against me. "My God!" I cried. "This is the worst yet! What's happened here? What's happened to the city?"

Over the vista broke a cold gray light, such as seen in those false dawns that are neither night nor true morning, when the world and all its contents seem but shapes of mist, formed of vain hope and desire... If you awake from troubled sleep at such a time, you can only sit by the window and think of those that have been lost to you, those that followed your parents into those cold and heartless regions below the grass, silent and dark. Eventually morning comes and the world resumes its solidity, but another tiny thread of ice has been stitched into your heart forever.

Such was the illumination by which I saw the ruins of London. But now they did not seem just freshly battered by war, but weathered away by passing centuries. The heaps of rubble had lost their jagged edges, sinking under mould and decaying vegetation. The road was cracked and riven, as though the Earth beneath was shrinking with age. As I surveyed the appalling scene a small, shiny-black thing like a salamander darted to the crest of one low mound, glared at us with eyes like two pin-points of light, then darted away. Another one, but with inky bat wings, flapped up from one of the street's cracks, then curved away on the chilling breeze that came from the west.

"Not a pretty sight, eh, Hocker." Ambrose lifted his walking stick and pointed with it to the horizon. "This is the way it is all the way to the ocean, and in all the lands beyond as well."

"My God," I said. "What have you brought me to? Is this some future time when Man and Morlock both have rotted away? What comes after this, for God's sake?"

"Nothing comes after this, actually," said Ambrose briskly. "And nothing before, either. Your good, comfortable year of 1892 and all the other years of Victoria's reign, and all the rest of the Earth's existence from its gaseous birth to its final fiery plunge back into the sun, are no more. What you see around you are the rocks and shoals of Eternity after the Sea of Time has been drained away. Such is the final upshot of all that mucking about with Time Travel."

"You don't mean—" I stammered. "Surely not— surely this isn't the end of it all." The scene's oppressive gloom weighed heavier and heavier upon me.

"My dear fellow," said Ambrose mildly, "this is no *end* to everything, this *is* everything. The

Alpha and Omega of the Earth's existence. Nothing but this through all Time, Past and Present – if those words still meant anything."

"But how?" I seized his arm in desperation. "How could it, have happened?"

"You yourself ate dinner with the man who built the Time Machine, and heard his story. Even such a trifling little excursion as his was in fact so gross a violation of the Universe's natural order as to make distant galaxies warp from their courses! That such power ever fell, however unwittingly, into a mortal man's control was no license for him to actually go and use it. And then when the Morlocks gained control of the Time Machine, and sent whole armies trooping back and forth between your century and theirs – can't you imagine what happened? A temporal implosion! Our little pocket of the Universe was sucked out of the flow of Time and into this dark, unchanging abyss."

His language and manner of speaking had become more vehement, breaking through the cool demeanour with which he had first addressed me. Evidently the sight of the Earth forsaken by Time – and God? – affected him more deeply than he had wished to show.

"Then what are we to do?" I cried. "If Time no longer exists – are we to stay like this without end?" I could conceive of no more cheerless hell than being condemned to this wretched spot.

"Well, Mr. Hocker," said Dr. Ambrose, again smiling. "Of all the questions that a man can ask, I do love that one. What are we to do? The best question that can ever be asked, indeed. Because you must know *what* to do before you can *do* it. Eh? Don't you think so, my good Hocker?"

"For God's sake, you torment me with these riddles." Anger and indignation filled my breast, as I felt he was making mock of me. "If you know of some way of escaping this dreadful place, show it to me. I've near gone out of my head as it is from all you've done to me. To me, and to – Tafe!" A pang of guilt struck me as I realised I had forgotten the companion who had saved my life. "Where is she?" I demanded. "What's happened to her?"

"Calm down, Hocker. The woman's perfectly safe. I've tended her injuries and deposited her in a warm bed, elsewhere. You'll have to inform me of all the adventures you two had together."

"Elsewhere!" I grabbed him by both shoulders and spun him roughly about to face me. "Elsewhere! There's no end to your damned lies. This isn't the final doom of the Earth, then, is it?"

"But it is, Hocker." He casually brushed my hands away from himself. "This is the Earth when Time no longer exists for it. But you asked for a way out? Perhaps, Hocker, perhaps. Not an escape exactly but... a prevention. A thwarting."

"What do you mean?"

"If this," said Ambrose, striking the ground with his walking stick, "is what remains when the Sea of Time – let's call it that, it's a nice metaphor – when the Sea of Time, as I say, has been drained away. Then obviously the thing to do is to go back and dam the hole through which it escaped. Eh? Doesn't it strike you that way?"

"I don't know." I felt suddenly weary. "I'm not sure I understand you. So much has happened. I'm very tired..."

"That's understandable," soothed Dr. Ambrose's voice. "Why don't you go to sleep?"

"I'd like to," I murmured. The vista around us seemed to darken.

"Then just close your eyes. That's it," came his voice, a little fainter. "Don't worry about falling. You're not really standing upright anyway, are you?"

Dimly, I was aware I was lying on a bed. The soft yellow glow of a gas lamp seeped under my eyelids for a second, then was gone. "Where's Tafe?" I mumbled.

"She's upstairs." Ambrose's voice was far away now. "Don't worry about her. Just sleep, Hocker. You're going to need all the strength you can summon very soon!"

The last I heard was the sound of a door being pulled shut.

I awoke with a calm, rested heart although my sleep had been full of nightmares. Visions of dark shapes moving in a dark world blurred and faded behind my eyes.

On a small table beside the bed in which I lay – and where in Creation was that? my refreshed mind was already wondering – I found a box of safety matches and a candle. I soon discovered my clothes draped across the ornately carved foot of the bed. They had through some miracle been restored to their original condition, clean and untorn.

I dressed quickly and hurried from the

bedchamber. A murmur of distant voices led me down a short hallway to a wide staircase. The warm glow of gaslight diffused upward from the room at the base of the stairs. I snuffed the candle and descended.

Seated at a heavy oak table were Dr. Ambrose and a young man. Only when I was standing at the side of the table did I recognise the young man to be no man at all, but Tafe outfitted in a man's suit and collar. The elegant cut and the confidence with which she wore it all served to disguise her femininity from anyone who was not aware of her true status. She pulled a thick black cigar from her mouth and winked at me through a cloud of tobacco smoke. The only sign of her recent wounds was a white line, as of a long healed cut, beneath her jaw.

"Hocker," said Ambrose genially, "glad to see you up and about. Great things are afoot, me lad, and I want you to be in for your full share of them. Have a chair."

From between the table's legs, carved into griffins, I drew a seat and joined them. Ambrose pushed a platter of roast beef, steaming from the blood-red centre of its slices, coarse bread and a glass of dark lager toward me.

"Much explaining to be done," he said, "and it would sit poorly on an empty stomach."

In truth, I was famished and needed little persuasion. Ambrose refilled my glass when it was only half drained. "From a little alehouse in the Berkshire moors," he noted, stoppering the jug. Tafe leaned back in her chair and drew luxuriously on her cigar with all the aspect of one sunk fast into the grip of some new-found pleasure.

"Mmm. Yes. Quite good, really," I managed to say between mouthfuls. "Surely you're having some?"

"We've dined already," said Ambrose, waving a hand at a pair of dirty dishes at the other end of the table. "Miss Tafe – or Mister Tafe, as I should say for the sake of her little masquerade – and I have been waiting some time for you to appear."

"I'm sorry to have kept you, but I was as tired as I've ever been in–" I broke off, scowling at my plate as I sensed the absurdity of the situation. Only a little while ago I had been scrabbling about for my life in a battle-torn cityscape into which I had been thrust by this mysterious personage's doing, then shown a soul-chilling glimpse of the Earth's

end, and now I was enjoying the warm
amenities of his home as calmly as if it had
all been some weekend visit. If nothing else,
it demonstrated the human mind's facility
for landing poised as a cat in unfamiliar situ-
ations and making the best of them. And
who indeed could turn down good ale and
meat, though it were served by the Devil
himself? I resolved to hear out my odd host's
explanations and judge him for good or evil
on the basis thereof.

Ambrose, all genial hospitality, extended
across the ruins of my meal a box of cigars
such as the one Tafe was smoking. I took one
and slipped off a paper band with some Ara-
bic- looking gibberish inscribed on it. Soon
the three of us were hazing the air with
steel-grey smoke.

"Where to begin," mused Ambrose, gazing
up into the swirling nimbus. "*Doing* is always
so much easier than *explaining*. See here,
Hocker," he said, pointing the glowing
ember of his cigar at me. "Doesn't the name
'Dr. Ambrose' seem a little... *suspicious* to
you? Eh?"

"My dear sir," I said coolly, laying a flake of
ash in my plate, "everything about you seems

suspicious. If I had no knowledge of your abilities I would maintain you to be either a charlatan or a lunatic. As it is, you might still be a rogue or a master criminal, but one of sufficient accomplishments to be respected."

He nodded, modestly restraining his pleasure at my flattery. "But come," he said, gesturing with his cigar. "How about the name 'Ambrosius', then? In connection with early British history?"

I frowned in deep thought. "I'm a reasonably well-educated man," I said at last, "but at the moment the only reference to an 'Ambrosius' I can recall is that of Geoffrey of Monmouth giving it as an alternate name for the legendary Merlin—"

"That's the one," he interrupted.

"Well, Dr. Ambrose, if you've chosen to derive your pseudonym from that of a mythical magician, I must admit that in your case it's appropriate."

"Mythical!" He glared irritably at me. "Legendary! Sir Geoffrey may have gotten some of his dates wrong but at least everything I told him was true. No, don't say anything stupid." He waved my protests off with his cigar. "I won't prolong your ignorance. I call myself 'Ambrose' because I dislike the effete Latinism of 'Ambrosius', but in fact I am the actual Merlin himself! What do you think of that?" His voice reached an exultant peak as he dramatically flourished his cigar.

I puffed away on my own, unable to say anything for sheer bafflement. Merlin, indeed. The man was mad. But, still...

"I believe it," announced Tafe complacently.

"That, my dear," said Ambrose, "is because you grew up in a rough and violent world where just managing to live from day to day is easily considered a miracle. You are able to accept the truth, no matter how astonishing its guise. Whereas our friend Hocker here is steeped in the overweening rationalism of his time, and could mentally dismiss a mastodon in front of him if it happened to be wearing the wrong school tie."

"Actually," said Tafe, "I just kind of figured – why not? Makes as much sense as anything else so far."

"But see here!" I exploded. "How could it possibly be? Even if such a person as Merlin existed centuries ago, how could you be that person? I mean your... whole appearance, for one thing."

"Why should someone with powers such as mine ever age? I was old when England was nothing but bare rocks washed by the sea." Ambrose's eyes seemed to look through me and into some vast repository of memory. "Believe what I tell you! *I am that one called Merlin, though even that is not the oldest or truest of my names.* Damn your sceptical eyes, man – what more do you need to see before you accept the truth?"

The low-pitched intensity of his voice quite unnerved me. And what other explanation had I for the mystifying tangle I had fallen into? None other than the possibility of my own insanity. "I'll accept your assertion of identity – provisionally," I said. "At least for the balance of your story,"

Another fierce glare from his dark eyes before he leaned back in his chair and continued. "There is a certain spiritual power," he said quietly, "inherent in the English blood and soil. An embodiment of the highest Western values. This power, of course, gets perverted or eclipsed from time to time. A lot of this jingo nonsense going on in the name of Empire isn't much of a credit to the English race. But still, it's only a temporary lapse of memory. *The power remains*, however tarnished or neglected it becomes. And I have, shall we say, an interest in preserving that. For if it should die, the world would darken and lapse into brutishness. And I would be alone upon the face of the Earth. Now, as many times in the past, that spiritual power is threatened with destruction."

"You mean, the Morlocks," I interjected.

"Ah, so you accept that much?"

"I've seen them."

"True, true," said Ambrose, nodding. "And such was largely the point of your recent harsh experiences. I could conceive of no other way to convince you that things are as I asked you to speculate when I first talked to you that evening in the fog. The Time Machine does exist, and has fallen in the hands of the Morlocks."

"And our host of that evening?" I said. "The inventor of the Machine?"

"Dead, I'm afraid. He thought that a rifle and a case of matches would be enough to establish his will in that far future. Unfortunately, as I told you, the Morlocks he encountered the first time were the least to be feared of their kind."

"And now they are secretly invading our own present-day London and all England beyond that." My calm statement of the fact belied the fear and revulsion it produced in my heart.

"Indeed," said Ambrose. "The Time Machine's inventor actually understood less about his device than he thought he did. By going between this time and that of the Morlocks he created a channel from which no deviation is possible. This time, and no other, is the only one to which the Morlocks could travel with their new device. They can only launch their invasion through this one point in their past, our own year 1892."

"Wait a moment," I said, frowning and turning his words about in my mind. "There's something wrong here... I've got it. If the Morlocks come back in Time to their own past and wreak such havoc, aren't they endangering the chain of events that lead to their own existence? Why, they might be conquering and then eating their own ancestors! And thus obliterating their own nasty lives scores of generations before their own births!" The topsy-turvy logic of it all boggled me for a moment, and I puffed furiously on my cigar.

Ambrose graciously inclined his head. "I admire your astuteness, Hocker. Not many of your contemporaries could follow that, let alone come up with it themselves. Indeed, it *is* a violation of the Universe's natural order. This whole business of Time Travel is shot through with cosmic blasphemy, I'm afraid. Better to take the years as they come one by one on the string, instead of mucking about and yanking on the thread to see what's coming. Be that as it may. The paradox of the Morlocks eating their own distant forefathers is relatively minor compared to the catastrophe that threatens the Earth through their mere use of the Time Machine. And that catastrophe is the implosion of Time itself, just as you saw, Hocker, before I brought you here. The year 1892 has become the hole through which the Sea of Time is leaking away. Even as we sit here the events of the years before and after this date are blurring into our own time. If the process is not halted and reversed, soon all Time from the Earth's beginning to its end will run together into one year, then contract into a single day, a minute, second, then – like that! Blink out of existence. Leaving that dark, timeless desert you found yourself in."

"Good God!" I cried. "If this is true—"

"It is."

"—then what can we do to stop it from happening? If, as you say, the Morlocks have already torn open this hole in the cosmos, how can we mend it?" A chilling thought struck me. "Or is it too late even now, and you only mean to horrify us with your prevision of the Earth's end?"

"Calm down, Hocker." Ambrose flicked another ash into his plate. "What would be the point of a needless torment such as that? If evil weren't preventable – and this one in particular – I wouldn't waste time talking to people like you."

I felt a flush of anger suffuse my face. "What is to be done, then?" I demanded. "I'll accept everything you've said so far if you'd round it off with a plan of action."

"Spoken like a true Englishman, Hocker! Hot for blood and violence – an admirable quality indeed."

"It's not that," I said tentatively, feeling my way through my own thoughts. "It's just that that the evil of it is all so strong."

Ambrose nodded, sober-faced. "Yes," he said quietly. "Something so large as this... When I first talked with you, so long ago it seems even to me, what was it said? Do you recall your words?"

"Truthfully, no."

"*It took an Arthur to drive out the Saxons in the Fifth Century. It would take another hero such as that to fight fiends like the Morlocks... and where is such an Arthur Redivivus to be found?*" Those were very perceptive words, Hocker. An intuitive grasp of the situation. Arthur Redivivus, indeed. Well put, that."

"Come, come," I said. "I'm well aware of the stories concerning King Arthur and his return from his death-like sleep whenever England is threatened, but that's all myths, and legends, and... hmm..."

"Myths and legends," said Ambrose, smiling wickedly. "The same as Merlin, I suppose? I'm flattered to sense that you've come to accept my true identity, but why should you pull short of the whole truth?"

My eyes flicked from his face to Tafe's impassively listening countenance, and back again. "King Arthur is alive?"

"Most assuredly."

"And you know where he is?"

"Of course," said Ambrose. "His and my destinies are much intertwined. I always know where he is."

"And–" My mind raced with possibilities. "And he's prepared to lead some sort of armed expeditionary force against the Morlocks?"

"Not quite. There's, ah, *difficulties* involved, shall we say."

Through the thick, stratifying layers of cigar haze I gazed at the enigmatic figure across from me. Could all he had said be true? What hope was there if it turned out to be lies? *King Arthur lives...* "Can we go to him?" I said. "See him?" I still had many questions, many points I did not yet understand, but I was willing to let those ride for the moment.

"Let us find a hansom outside," said Ambrose, rising from the table. "He's here in the very city of London itself."

Stepping outside of Dr. Ambrose's lodgings gave me my first sight of London since those nightmarish scenes of destruction and despair. My heart leaped to see the familiar outlines, whole and unbroken, silhouetted against the setting sun. Lamps were being lit all over the city to show the glowing pulse of a great metropolis in the full stretch of its powerful life. But if Ambrose's words were true, were there not even now dark things moving in the undispelled shadows? The very ground beneath our feet was being eaten away...

Soon Dr. Ambrose had hailed a hansom and, after giving directions to the river, assisted Tafe and myself inside. "I shall meet you at your destination," he said, standing on the curb. "Circumstances dictate that I follow a more circuitous route." He closed the hansom's door and signalled the driver on his topside ledge into motion.

How easily Tafe seemed to be taking this all in her stride! Child of a time more than one generation hence, she sat in the hansom's slightly tattered elegance, looking for all the world like some young Continental buck with no greater business to follow than seeing England on a grand tour organised by rich parents. Through the hansom's window she watched the passing cityscape and evening pedestrians with avid curiosity but no signs of being startled or amazed by any of it. Those responses had been denied her at birth by the swift and violent tenor of her own times.

"I say, Tafe," I addressed her. "What do you think of this Ambrose fellow? How much of what he's been telling us do you suppose is true?"

She turned to face me, her dark, intelligent eyes flashing from her mannish disguise like a young George Sand. There was clearly a keen wit in addition to the fighting spirit I had already had the chance to observe. "Ambrose?" she said. "Might be lying through his teeth for all we know. But what choice do we have except to follow along with him for now? If he's telling the truth about all these Morlocks and stuff then we've got to help him in whatever he's planning. And if he's lying, using us for something evil – aiding the Morlocks, maybe? – we'll have a better chance of fighting him if he thinks we trust him."

Her calm, unemotional analysis preoccupied my thoughts. I lapsed into silence, mulling over her words to the rhythm of the cabhorse's hooves, while she went back to watching the passing London scene.

Soon enough the hansom halted and we alighted. The driver, already paid his fare by

Dr. Ambrose, rattled off. Looking about us, I recognised the building in front of us. I had observed it several times before on my various peregrinations about the city. Prompted by idle curiosity, I had even inquired in some nearby shops as to the building's nature, for it was a quite imposing modern edifice, set behind a high iron fence and well-groomed lawns. Yet seemingly it was inhabited only by an aged caretaker who saw that no street urchins or burglars penetrated its shuttered windows and thus gained access to its unlit interior. The local shopkeepers rumoured it to be a private clinic established by some wealthy foreign physician who had yet to make his appearance and begin his practice.

Things had apparently changed since last I had seen the building, for now the windows were all brightly lit up. As Tafe and watched from the street, the silhouetted figure of a nurse in her starched cap passed across one of the lower windows.

"I wonder what he sent us here for," said Tafe. "And where is he?"

Indeed, the mysterious Dr. Ambrose was nowhere to be seen. "Perhaps he has been delayed," I conjectured. "By whatever it was that necessitated his travelling separately."

"Well, we can't just stand around here." Tafe started walking along the high iron fence that surrounded the clinic's grounds. I followed her and within a few paces we found ourselves in darkness beyond the reach of the street lamps that graced the street in front of the building.

"Pssst! Hocker, Tafe – over here!" I turned and saw Ambrose's form separate from the deepest shadows along the fence. He beckoned us toward him. "Cheerful business, what?" he said when the three of us had formed a little conspiratorial knot against the iron railings.

"Why have you brought us here?" I asked, keeping my voice low. "What's our business got to do with some private clinic?"

"You'll see." Ambrose drew a cylindrical object from beneath his cloak.. It was a ship captain's brass-bound telescope which he quickly extended to its full length. "Take a sight on that large window there," he said, handing the telescope to me.

I obliged, and soon had focused the glass upon the window Ambrose had pointed out.

The lenses were of excellent – or magical? – quality, revealing the room beyond the window pane in full detail.

"Well?" demanded Ambrose. "What do you see?"

"Hmm… I see a rather nicely appointed room, more like a drawing room of someone's home than a clinical facility. Books, fire on the grate, all that sort of thing. And an elderly man sitting in a wing chair, reading from a book." I passed the telescope to Tafe, who in turn focused it upon the window in question. "Is any of that important?" I asked.

"The man you see up there," said Ambrose coolly, "is none other than the reincarnated King Arthur, defender of Britain."

"But… but that's an old man in there!" I exclaimed. "Quite silver-haired!"

"Arthur has been born and grown old in many lives," said Ambrose. "Except those lives when he was cut down in the prime of his youth while performing his duty to England and all Christendom."

"But he's an old man *now*," I said. "What hope do we have of defeating the Morlocks with a champion like that?"

"Spoken like a snotty youngster," said Ambrose. "Old age is a great warrior's best time, when his military abilities are tempered with the truest wisdom. No, it's not Arthur's advanced years in this life that have weakened him and thus prevent him from leading the battle against the Morlocks. There are other factors at work here."

"Such as?"

"My dear Hocker, we are in the process of unravelling this mystery together. You and Tafe are my allies in piecing together a truth of which I possess only a few fragments. I know that Arthur is disastrously enfeebled at the present time, and I know who is responsible. But how it has been done and what we are to do about it are matters we are to discover jointly."

"I take it then," said I, "that Arthur is being held prisoner in this place? By whom?"

"Someone else just came into the room," said Tafe with her eye to the telescope. She peered intently at the lighted window for several more seconds, then murmured, "This is incredible. It looks like–"

"Let me see." I took the telescope from her willing hand and focused on the room's

interior. "By God!" I exclaimed. "It– it is you!"
I lowered the telescope and whirled upon
Ambrose. "The man talking to Arthur is the
exact twin of you! What's going on here?"

Without a word of explanation, Ambrose
took the telescope from me and gazed at the
two figures revealed through the window,
the grey but still noble-looking old man and
the unnervingly exact double of Ambrose
himself. "Yes," he murmured, taking the telescope from his eye and collapsing it to its
smallest form. "You've seen him. An old
nemesis of mine, of all humanity to be exact;
roused to activity again by this fiendish
Time-juggling of the Morlocks."

"But who – or what – is he?"

"He is now going under the name of Dr.
Merdenne, of Paris, the founder and head
surgeon of his private clinic here in London.
But I have known him in other times and
places far removed from this. Perhaps the
high point of his many previous careers was
when he was known as Ibrahim, high counsellor to the Great Suleiman, back in the days
when the Ottoman Empire was at its zenith
and a constant menace to Christian Europe.
Arthur and I both struggled with him then,

and narrowly averted the defeat and extinction of all Christendom."

"This Merdenne is immortal, then – like you."

Ambrose's eyes narrowed to slits as he continued his gaze at the distant window. "Immortal, yes," he said. "But not like me. Merdenne – for so shall we call him now, as his true name should never be pronounced – is a caricature of myself and my powers, dedicated to a lust for evil dominion over men. But not as their ruler. Rather he lies dormant in the bowels of the Earth until an opportunity arises to manipulate in secret those of brutal and domineering ambitions. Thus he was Suleiman's counsellor, and now has thrown his wiles behind the Morlocks, with the dark hope of making himself the secret power behind their rule of all Time. He, even more than the Morlocks themselves, is our cruellest and most implacable enemy – subtle and with powers great as my own." Ambrose fell silent, gazing with unreadable emotions at the lighted window and the two small figures beyond the glass.

A cold wind swirled around us, and I shivered. Ambrose glanced at me sharply.

"Yes," he said. "You're right. Here in the darkness is no place to speak of things like this. Let us find a little warmth and human noise in which to shelter ourselves. Dark secrets and plans will lead to dark actions soon enough."

He led us to a small pub a few streets away, where the stout proprietor in his stained apron nodded to Ambrose as if he were a long-familiar customer. Soon three of Ambrose's excellent cigars were turning the air blue in a booth at the rear of the pub, as we worked our way down through a pitcher of dark beer.

"It's like this," said Ambrose. The glowing tip of his cigar danced in the smoky haze. "King Arthur is reborn every generation in time to intercede against the direst threat facing the cherished Christian and human ideals that are embodied in England more than any other place. It's a commentary on humanity's penchant for mischief, inasmuch as there's *always* a threat to Christendom. Evil exists on its own but the best and brightest must be guarded as though they were but flickering candle flames; Hence Arthur and his cycle of lives and deaths.

"But–" His cigar jabbed at us. "It's more complicated than just that. The Fates have their little jokes and trials for us all. Arthur lives again and again, but each time he is born he has no memory of being Arthur. He grows into manhood – coward, fool, or even a hero – unaware that he is England's greatest defender called forth in her time of need."

"Then of what use is his being Arthur?" I said. "If he lives as no more than any other man, good or bad – of what good is his other true self that is locked away?"

"Quite right, Hocker. Very perceptive." Ambrose drew long and meditatively upon his cigar. "Locked away indeed – but there is a key."

I glanced over at Tafe but her expression remained unchanged behind her own veil of exhaled smoke.

"The key is Excalibur," said Ambrose quietly. "Arthur's sword, though it is much older than even he. Its power has diminished since the long distant age when Arthur's ancestor Fergus chopped mountains in two with it. But it is still a weapon of great strength, and more than that. Every time Arthur dies, Excalibur returns into the earth and is lost –

until it finds its way into the hands of one who can read the inscription on its blade and doing so, knows that he is not the person he thought he was, that the name he bore is not his true one, that he is in fact Arthur Pendragon, the defender of England. Sword and key – Excalibur is both."

"That is all very well, I'm sure," said I, "but where is this magical weapon at the present moment? I trust you know of its whereabouts."

"Not so simple as that, Hocker." Ambrose's lean face darkened with his inner thoughts. "Arthur was reincarnated in this life as one Henry Morsmere – now Brigadier-General Morsmere – after a long and minorly distinguished military career – and found the sword Excalibur somewhere in the smoking aftermath of one of the Crimean battlefields. I was watching him from behind the blackened remnant of a tree and saw him stoop down at the sight of his seemingly accidental discovery. When he stood back up with the blade in his hands I could see that he had read the inscription and that he knew who he truly was. No longer General Morsmere, but Arthur. His eyes were as dark as wells with the memories of the many lives and accumulated centuries through which he's been."

"Just like that, eh?" said I. "He remembers everything?"

Ambrose nodded. "In an instant it happens and he is transformed. The inscription on Excalibur's blade is formed in an ancient runic script. The reading of these words summons up Arthur's real identity to his mind. I saw it happen on that Crimean battlefield as I had seen it happen many times before, but I did not reveal myself to him then, though he would certainly have recognised me as his trusted adviser and friend. Things were not yet at a stage where his intervention was needed. Soon enough that messy, blundering business in the Crimea was ended, and Arthur – still posing for convenience's sake as General Morsmere – returned to England, retired from his military status and took a suite at the Savoy to await the coming of the task for which he had been summoned to life again. He kept Excalibur hidden under a false bottom of his old military campaign chest"

"I see." The image occupied me of Gen. Morsmere/Arthur sitting alone in his hotel suite, patiently waiting for the danger to England to appear for which he had been summoned to life again. Sometimes, no doubt, he must have taken Excalibur from his chest's secret compartment and lightly ran a whetstone down its gleaming length. And other times he very likely looked out the window upon our bustling, modern and prosperous world, and thought – ah, what would he have thought? For some reason I couldn't imagine this proud old warrior-king looking upon the scene with much satisfaction. I cut short my melancholy musing and returned my attention to Ambrose's exposition.

"So," he continued, with another wave of his cigar, "when I became at last aware of the grim situation with the Morlocks – for with my old adversary's guidance they had managed to conceal themselves from my notice until their invasion plans were well underway – I then hied myself to Arthur's pied-a-terre in order that we could formulate together a strategy to roust the Morlocks from their toehold in the London sewers of this time. But when I arrived at his Savoy suite I discovered not Arthur, but–" He broke off to take a quick pull at his beer.

"Who was it?" I interjected.

"No one." Grey flakes of ash floated down to the table. "No one at all. Arthur was gone. None of the hotel staff had seen General Morsmere, as they knew him, for several days. Inveigling myself into his suite, I found that Excalibur was missing as well from the secret compartment in Morsmere's chest."

"Abducted!" I cried. "Abducted by this opponent of yours who now calls himself Merdenne."

"Quite right, Hocker, as I soon found out through my own sources. I have a large network of people who, through friendship, fear or finance, manage to keep an eye on most things that happen in London for me. One such informant quickly discovered Arthur's whereabouts – Merdenne's clinic." Which was also the first revelation to me that my old adversary was involved in all this."

"But I don't understand," said I. "If, as you say, Arthur's fighting prowess is undiminished by age and he was in possession of his miraculous Excalibur as well, how were his abductors able to overpower him and bear him off to Merdenne's clinic? Surely he would at least have put up enough of a struggle to alarm the management of the Savoy. And by what deviltry is he kept a hapless prisoner in the clinic?"

"Those are mysteries, Hocker, that are quite deeper than my present knowledge." Ambrose's eyes darkened with brooding. "Many answers will depend upon your getting Arthur out of Merdenne's grasp."

I glanced across at Tafe and saw that even her eyes had widened a bit in surprise. "What was that," said I to Ambrose, "about getting Arthur out of the clinic?"

"Yes, well, quite frankly, it's going to be up to you and Tafe. That's the whole point of my enlisting you as my allies. It would be disastrous for me even to attempt to enter the clinic. The automatic result would be my death and an enormous increase in Merdenne's own power. The very building itself is a trap designed to leech off my spiritual power and transfer it to Merdenne. No, as I said, the task falls to you and Tafe – to enter the clinic, find both Arthur and Excalibur, and bring them both out again."

"But surely," I protested, "if Merdenne can devise a trap such as that for you, no doubt even worse pitfalls await lesser figures such as we two. What better chance would Tafe and I have in such a place."

"No chance at all," said Ambrose placidly. "The only exit you would make would be as cinders and ashes rising out of one of the clinic's chimneys, and the Morlock's invasion plans would continue apace. True enough are your forebodings – *if* Merdenne were to be aware of your having entered the clinic."

"And what's to prevent that? Surely the place is rigged with alarms enough to warn him of any surreptitious visitors."

"Indeed so, Hocker. You anticipate my every precaution. But alarms, effective as they might ordinarily be, are of little avail to someone who is, shall we say, too distracted to hear them."

"You propose, then, to divert Merdenne's attention while Tafe and I invade his stronghold and liberate Arthur? How, pray, do you intend to do that?" A touch of sarcasm entered my voice, increased by my anxiety over the whole project.

"That," said Ambrose, "is my concern. You needn't worry over it."

"And what should happen if your ploy fails and Merdenne discovers the invasion before we are quit of the premises? What then?"

"Then, Hocker, he will hideously murder you and Tafe, hide Arthur in some new place beyond my powers of discovery, and all will be lost. It is as simple as that."

"Oh." My cigar had gone out, and I pulled disconsolately at the dead stub.

"Well, Hocker?" said Ambrose after a moment's silence on all our parts. "I can't very well force you to help in a matter like this."

"I suppose not. Still – one never really plans on encountering this sort of thing."

"Show a little backbone," said Tafe. They were the first words she had spoken since we had entered the pub. "Things will get pretty rotten soon enough if you don't do anything at all. You saw what it'll be like. At least this way we've got a chance of preventing all that."

Shamed at this rebuke from a woman, I nodded. "When do we start?" I dropped the cigar stub to the littered floor and ground it beneath my boot heel.

"Capital," said Ambrose. "We haven't a moment to lose. Listen…"

Tafe and I leaned our heads closer toward him. I followed the outlines of his plan, while the cowardly portion of my heart turned away and fled.

4
In the Clinic

*"Ah, my dear... Merdenne. Mind if I join you?"
His pale hand was already drawing back the chair
on the other side of the table.*

*"Why, Ambrose – it's still Ambrose, isn't it? –
of course not. Here, do try some of the Latour." The
one called Merdenne took one of the unused wine
glasses above his plate, poured the lustrous red
vintage into it, and extended it across the restaurant's snowy-white damask.*

*"Thank you." Ambrose held the glass to the
light, then brought it to his nose and inhaled
deeply, then at last drank of it, rolling the wine on
his tongue to savour it fully. "Quite pleasant," he
said after a moment's reflection. "But the vintners
really should, have asked for a priest's blessing on
that old graveyard before they planted their vines
in it. The unconsecrated bones in the soil leave, I*

fear, a bitter aftertaste in the mouth."

"Actually," said Merdenne with a thin smile, *"that's the thing I like most about this wine."*

Ambrose half-smiled back. *"De gustibus non disputandum. Not your usual sort of refreshment anyway, is it? You were fond of a rather different intoxicant, I believe, when you were a counsellor to the great Suleiman."*

Across the width of the restaurant, one waiter nudged another in the ribs and pointed at the two men. "Look at em," he whispered to his colleague. "Just as like as two eggs in the same nest!" The other nodded in sage acknowledgment. "Those are what are called identicable twins," he pronounced with grave authority.

Merdenne took a swallow from his own glass. "One must conform," he said, "to the vices of the time and place one finds one's self in. I'm afraid this England of which you're so fond isn't quite civilised enough yet to view the open smoking of opium without at least a small measure of scandal. Though I imagine the scandal lies more in the lower class associations of the habit, rather than in any perceived peril in the drug itself. How tiresome these little minds are, with their endless preoccupations about classes, places and positions! Won't you be glad to see them all wiped away at last?"

"Twins or no," said the first waiter, "there's something about the sight of the two of em sitting together that fair makes me blood creep! What do you suppose they could ever be talking about?"

"They might," said Ambrose coolly, "not be wiped away as easily as you fancy."

"Come, come, Ambrose. Don't delude yourself. In the past, our conflicts have been like... like chess games, so to speak. Yes, exactly, games of chess. But in this one, your king is already forfeited to me. Check and mate. The game is over. Nothing is left but the clearing of the pieces from the board."

"Perhaps, perhaps... You speak of chess. I would imagine you've found few opponents hereabouts worthy of your passion for that game!" Ambrose sipped at his wine, letting his eyes wander over the crowded restaurant. The noise of many conversations, the clink of silverware on china, all washed against the two of them.

"Damn, but you're right enough about that," said Merdenne fervently. "This is a nation of whist players, and other beastly card games which serve as nothing more than a pretext for polite gabbling at the opposite sex!"

"Not at all the sort of chess-playing opportunities you had when you were known as Ibrahim, I suppose."

"Nothing like," said Merdenne. "Even Suleiman himself was an avid player, though inclined not to value his pawns sufficiently. How I miss those days! Studying the chessboard through a haze of opium smoke, as if one were an eagle floating miles above the desert, scrutinising the affairs of men… master of all…" He lapsed into a silent reverie.

"See here, Merdenne. I'll stand you a game."

"Would you really?" His eyes brightened. "That's beastly good of you, Merlin – pardon, I mean Ambrose. Considering that you've lost just about everything on the outs."

Ambrose cleared the bottle of Latour and the wine glasses from the centre of the table. From his coat pocket he brought a little cube of enamelled wood that, with a click of springs and hinges, expanded into a small chessboard. Thirty-two small figures in black and white spilled from felt-lined pockets on the board's underside.

"That's a clever item," said Merdenne admiringly. "Your own design?"

"Yes." Ambrose shuffled two of the pieces about in his hands, then extended his closed fists across the table. Merdenne hesitated before tapping one of his opponent's fists. "Just a game, right?" he said cautiously. "You won't win here what you've lost on the larger board – the world, that is."

Ambrose nodded. "Just a game." He opened the fist that Merdenne then tapped, revealing the White Queen. "Your move."

The pieces were quickly arranged in their places, and Merdenne pushed his queen's pawn forward. Ambrose met it with his own, but before Merdenne could continue his opening, a crash of dinnerware sounded beside the table.

"Excuse me, sirs," mumbled a red-faced waiter, gathering up his spilled tray. "Don't know what I come to stumble over." He shot a suspicious glance at Ambrose's feet, but they were both under the table once more.

Merdenne looked annoyed as his hand moved toward one of his knights. "Not exactly the most conducive atmosphere for concentration," he muttered. "Suleiman would have had the noisy lout beheaded."

"The noise at least is easily taken care of." Ambrose closed his eyes, drew a deep breath and held it. When he exhaled and opened his eyes the restaurant was empty except for the two of them. Silence flowed over the unoccupied chairs.

"That's quite thoughtful of you," said Merdenne. "Now we can have a proper game. Finish off the Latour, if you wish."

Ambrose's pale hand tilted the bottle over his

glass, but only a whisper of dry dust emerged. His opponent didn't notice.

"Now where'd they go?" said the waiter who had first noticed them. "Them two look-alikes, I mean. I'm blowed if they haven't up and vanished!"

"So?" said the other. "It's not one of your tables, is it?"

I drew out my pocket watch and checked the time. "Ambrose has been gone for half an hour," I whispered to Tafe.

She nodded, standing beside me in the dark alley that ran alongside Merdenne's clinic. From under her coat she drew the coil of rope Ambrose had given us to use. As I followed her to the railings of the high iron fence surrounding the clinic's grounds, I fervently hoped that Ambrose's plans for diverting Merdenne's attention had gone off smoothly. The sight of Ambrose's uncanny double leaving an hour ago for his favourite restaurant as we crouched in our hiding place in the alley had unnerved me more than slightly. As Tafe and I had waited per Ambrose's instructions, the dark shape of the clinic had seemed to grow ever larger as it sat hulking under the moonless sky.

Tafe threw the rope's looped end over one of the fence's sharp-pointed finials, then deftly clambered up and dropped on the other side. A little more clumsily, my hands barely keeping purchase on the rope's knotted length, I came after her, landing ungracefully upon the manicured lawn.

"Quiet!" whispered Tafe. We huddled by the fence for several anxious seconds, until we were sure that no one in the clinic had heard us. "Come on." Tafe jerked the rope free from the fence and wadded it under her coat again as she darted hunched-over toward the clinic.

She reached the side of the building without incident, but before I was more than halfway across the ground, a large shape, snarling viciously, bounded from the other side of a hedge and bowled me over. The red eyes of the largest mastiff I had ever seen glared at me as its slavering jaws snapped inches from my throat. The dog's spittle trailed in threads across my face. Pinned to the ground, only my forearms and knees brought above me kept the dog's lunging bulk away from its fatal goal. I knew, though, that only a few seconds more would leave me exhausted and open to the slashing teeth that strained toward me.

Suddenly, the beast's weight lifted from me and fell to one side. I rolled away from the scrabbling paws, then raised myself up to see Taft throttling the animal with the knotted rope. I quickly drew my breath, then threw myself alongside the desperately thrashing bodies of woman and animal, and clamped my hands about the mastiff's grimacing muzzle to prevent it from making any noise as it struggled.

Between us the dog could make no escape. and finally stiffened, then relaxed into death. A bubble of red burst through my fingers underneath the poor brute's white-rimmed eyes. We got to our feet and dragged its carcass with us into the complete darkness at the base of the clinic.

Valuable seconds had been lost in the struggle with the guard dog. Without waiting for us to gather our strength again, Tafe cast about for some means of forcing our way into the building. We both saw immediately that there was no way of gaining entry directly through the window of the room on the upper floor where Arthur was being held. There were no footholds available for climbing up to it, and no projections near the window itself sufficient for casting the rope upon. Tafe pointed to one of the windows of the darkened ground floor, indicating the route we had to follow.

From my belt I drew the short iron crowbar that Ambrose had furnished us, and handed it to Tafe. Whether the device had powers beyond those possessed by the ordinary burglar's tool I do not know, but combined with Tafe's manual dexterity it quickly snapped the window latch. She carefully pulled the window open, drew aside the drape on the other side, then lifted herself over the sill and into the unlit room.

I waited until she signalled for me to follow. Once inside, my ears detected the slight scraping noise of a patent safety match being struck. Tafe's face and hands, lit yellow by the match's sputtering glare, came into view. As the flame steadied and my eyes adjusted to the light, I could distinguish as well the outlines of the room – bare, except for some hastily stacked chairs and boxes in one corner. Tafe crossed to the closed door on the other side, with myself close behind. She put out the match before turning the knob.

With the door opened only an inch, we surveyed the interior of the building. The room we were in was adjacent to the clinic's grand foyer, lit by bare gas mantles along the walls. To the rear of the space a curving staircase led upstairs and to our captive goal. There was no indication of anyone in Merdenne's employ being about. While he, our greatest hazard, was, we hoped, distracted at the moment by our conspirator Ambrose, caution yet governed our moves, as the assistants to such evil – the human counterparts to the dead mastiff outside – could be dangerous enough to us and our plans. Slowly, Tafe drew the door open wide enough for us to slip through.

As we crossed the foyer, treading as lightly as possible, it was soon evident to us that Merdenne had not gone to any great effort to maintain his fiction of operating a medical clinic. The floor was made of rough, unfinished planks and the walls were rudely plastered by the workmen who had raised them. Obviously the landscaping outside the building was as thick a sham as Merdenne had felt necessary to fool the London public as to the nature of his operations in their midst.

We halted at the foot of the staircase. Tafe craned her neck, trying to peer up into the unlit gloom at its head. The steps curved away as they rose from the side of the building where Arthur's room lay. I wondered how circuitous a route we would have to follow in order to reach his room once we were upstairs.

Our moment of hesitation was broken by the sound of footsteps approaching the staircase from above. Tafe thrust her forearm across my chest and pushed me behind her into the shadow of the stairs' massive newel post.

From our hiding place we watched as a woman's shoes and skirts appeared at the head of the steps. She was dressed in a nurse's uniform, complete to the small cap made of starched linen set upon her tightly pulled-back hair. The images of comfort associated with her costume contrasted oddly with the forbidding aspect of her face – long, tight-lipped, with a cruel haughtiness about her slitted eyes. In her hands she carried a silver platter with the cold remnants of a barely touched meal upon it. Arthur's dinner? Be he general or warrior king, I could well understand a loss of appetite when served by a Hecuba like this one. Tafe and I both held our breaths as she descended the stairs.

The grim nurse reached the bottom step. Tafe darted from around the newel post and with her forearm got a throttlehold about the woman's neck. The loaded tray clattered to the floor, sending fragments of crockery across the wood planks. The woman's hands flew up to Tafe's arm and sank their nails into the flesh, but I managed to pull them away and pin them to her sides.

Tafe relaxed her hold a little. "How– how did you get in here?" gasped the woman. Her cold eyes, now flared wide, darted from my face to what she could see of Tafe over her shoulder. "What do you want?"

"Never mind how we got in," said Tafe grimly. "Who else is in the building with you? Working for Merdenne, that is?"

"If you're thieves, you've made a mistake. There's nothing of value here. Just look about you." The woman's mouth drew up into a sneer as she regained a measure of her composure.

Tafe lifted one knee into the small of the woman's back and pulled her into a bow. "I asked how many others like you were about."

"No... no one else," spoke the woman through pain-clenched teeth. Tafe let her straighten, and the blood flowed back into the woman's face.

"That's better," said Tafe. "Now you're going to lead us upstairs to the room where General Morsmere is being kept."

The woman glared at us, her face suffused with hatred. "You've made a grievous mistake to break in here." A gloating tone crept into her already harsh voice. "You're both as good as dead."

Her words chilled me – how was Ambrose's plan going? – but Tafe seemed unperturbed. "Don't bother stalling for time," she said evenly. "We've already taken care of your employer Merdenne. Don't you think that if he could do anything to stop our breaking in, he would've done it by now? But where is he? Eh?"

The woman's mouth tightened into a single bloodless line. Her eyes deepened with calculation. Like most agents of evil designs, her allegiances were transient and based on

personal advantage. Loyalty was an unknown concept. God knows what she
surmised the nature of our plans to be, but
it was obvious that Merdenne was rapidly
becoming a lesser factor in her own deci-
sions. "All right," she announced. "I'll take
you to Morsmere."

We bound her hands behind her with the
rope, then let her lead the way up the stairs.
As we gained the upper story it quickly became apparent that her presence in the
building had been a stroke of luck for us. The
corridor at the top of the stairs turned away
to the right, but the woman stepped up to the
blank wall on the left and trod upon a clev-
erly concealed latch at the base. A section of
the dark panelling slid away, and we followed
her into the passageway thus revealed.

"Here." She stopped and nodded her head
at a door.

Without saying a word, Tafe deftly kicked
the woman's feet from under her, lowered
her to the floor of the corridor, then trussed
her immobile with the rest of the rope. A
strip of cloth torn from the hem of the
nurse's uniform served as a gag. "Wait–" the
woman cried as Tafe wrapped it over her

mouth, then only her fiercely glaring eyes were able to finish her message.

I pushed the door open and surveyed the room beyond. At least Merdenne had had the graciousness to furnish it in keeping with the noble stature of his captive. Heavy drapes coursed down the burnished walls, while a tasteful collection of Persian miniatures were grouped over the carved fireplace. A pair of large humidors clad in Morocco leather stood on one side of the intricate Oriental carpets. Several hundred volumes similarly clad and stamped in gold on their bindings filled the library shelves.

A large wing chair was turned away from us toward the window, though I could see a man's hand, brown-spotted with age, resting upon one upholstered arm. I opened my mouth to speak, then halted in perplexity. How was I to address him? Morsmere or Arthur? General or king?

My dilemma was resolved when he, apparently having heard the door opening, twisted about in the chair and leaned over the arm to look, at us. "Yes?" he said. "What is it?"

The voice was deep, resonant with authority and command, the face lean and strong-boned,

with a high forehead below sparse grey hair.
Grey also was the neatly trimmed military
moustache. The eyes, deep set in his weathered
face, reflected a sombre, almost melancholy
nature, as though they were the repository of
some ancient, oft-repeated tragedy.

"I– we– that is…" My tongue moved in
confused stammering. "General Morsmere–"

"Please." He held up his hand. "There's
no need to maintain that fiction. Merlin
sent you, didn't he? Or Ambrose, as you
might know him. I've been expecting someone to come for some time now." His voice
seemed oddly weary, rather than pleased at
our arrival.

"That's right." I inclined my head in a bow
of respect. "My name is Edwin Hocker and my
companion here is called Tafe. That's all. We've
come to take your highness out of here."

"'Your highness'," he said, and sighed.
"Please don't burden yourself, Mr. Hocker,
with the empty trappings of courtly etiquette.
Arthur is all the name and title I ever wished."
He rose and faced us, clutching the chair's
arm for support. "And I'm afraid I must further disappoint you both. I don't think I'm
going to be leaving here."

"But, my dear sir, why not?" I stood dumb-founded at this development. Nothing was turning out as I had anticipated. Instead of being cheered at the prospect of his release, he seemed grimly displeased by it. "You know, don't you, that your England has need of you?"

"Merdenne – as he calls himself now – has gloatingly informed me of the whole situation." Arthur drew himself a little straighter. "It is not ignorance that keeps me here. No, not ignorance, but rather the opposite. I have not lived these many lives without re-membering something from each. And that knowledge wearies me." His old soldier's face seemed even older now, as though the skin were being pulled back toward the skull.

"What– what do you mean by that?" I suddenly felt chilled, as if a wind from some dark corner of the Earth had come into the room. From the corner of my eye I could see Tafe grow pale as well.

"I'm old," said Arthur. "Older than you could ever know. I've lived many times, and fought and died many times, and now I'm called to defend my England once more – but why?" The last word was a cry of bitterness breaking from his lips. "Did I live and die all those times so that a few children of England could grow fat while the many sweat out their drab lives in the dark holes of the cities?" His trembling hand flew toward the window, from which the dark shapes of the tenements could be seen. "And beyond our shores," he said with weary disgust. "Did I defend England so that other lands could be made to suffer our will, their people ground beneath our heel for our profit? Oh, how tarnished our English honour has become! How strong the armour that covers a rotted heart!" His mouth tightened below his burning eyes.

"But the Morlocks," I said in desperation. "Surely, even if everything you say is true, as many Englishmen themselves would agree, surely your land deserves a better fate than that!" Stirred by emotion, I crossed the room and gripped his arm – how frail it seemed! "That light – England's light is buried, but not gone out. Would you see it die forever?"

"If it did die," said Arthur quietly, "then this would be my final life, my final death, and I could rest at last."

I let go of him and drew away, my breast suddenly filled with anger and shame. "Then go to your rest!" I spat out. "Englishmen will fight and die without you, no matter how lost the cause." I turned from him, but before I could take a step my shoulder was grasped by his hand.

"Stay." His voice, though still melancholy, had a measure of, warmth in it. "I can see from you that that light is not so weak or buried so deep as I had feared." He went on as I faced him again. "If I was filled only with despair, how much easier it would be. But my heart still loves the green island beneath the dark spots of decay, my hands still raise to defend it. My bitter feelings would not be so strong if Merdenne had not contrived to weaken my nobler instincts."

"He has– enchanted you?" The recall of our adversary to my mind stiffened the skin along my arms.

Arthur nodded, turned and stepped – the shuffling stride of an old man! – toward the bookshelves. From its resting place atop a row of books he drew a long, cloth-wrapped bundle. "This is Excalibur," he said. "Merdenne leaves it with me as a taunt."

I took the bundle from his hands and unswaddled the weapon. A long blade, not ornate but impressively functional. Yet it seemed unnaturally light, as though made from some inferior metal. Disturbed by this sensation, I frowned as I studied the legendary sword. Tafe stepped up beside me and looked at it lying across my hands.

"There are runes," said Arthur. "Inscribed along the blade. From them I derive my knowledge of my true self, and the strength that accompanies that knowledge. Tell me what you see written there on the blade."

My eyes moved along the shining length of metal. "Why... they've faded!" I gasped. "The runes are hardly more than scratches! How could these be read?" I lifted my astonished gaze to his saddened face.

"Yes," he said mournfully. "How could they? This is Merdenne's work, and I fear it means the end of all England's hopes."

"But couldn't Ambrose do something about it? His power is as great as Merdenne's. Surely he could find some way of reversing whatever has been done to the sword."

Arthur slowly shook his head. "The power of Merlin is bound up with Excalibur's fate as well, though to a lesser degree. Merdenne has struck at us both through this damnable cleverness, and hobbled us beyond our capacities to set aright."

I shook my head and bent down to pick up the cloth at my feet. "What's done can be undone," I pronounced as I straightened up, sounding braver than I felt in my heart. "It's sad to see a noble weapon like this one degraded but if it can't be restored, then perhaps a Gatling artillery piece will serve as well to convince the Morlocks of their poor judgment."

A tired smile lit the old warrior's noble face. "Words fit for knighthood, my son, but—"

"Come." A desperate bravado had animated my spirits. I tucked the re-wrapped sword under one arm and grasped Arthur's elbow with my other hand. Tafe stepped to his side and caught his other arm, "My lord Arthur, we've dawdled here long enough. A little perambulation is good for the heart." Between us we nearly had him off his feet as we propelled him toward the door.

"Well," said Arthur, "I would like one more good lager before it's all too late. Merdenne serves the most wretched pale stuff."

"A fine idea." I said with all the heartiness I could muster. "On to the public house." My hand reached for the brass knob of the door–

He watched the movements of his opponent's hands with interest. "Castling?" said Dr. Ambrose in smiling reproach. "Surely that's a time-wasting defensive move, uncalled for at this point in a game. You should press your advantage. I'm already down two pawns."

Merdenne tapped his fingertips upon his king and one rook. "I must confess," he said, "that by strict logic you are correct. The nagging hunch I act upon is completely irrational. But all through the game I've had this compulsion to safeguard the king." He moved the pieces about to their new positions. "In the Orient, though, I learned that not all is dictated by logic." He leaned back in his chair and regarded the board.

A moment of silence passed in the room, empty except for the two chess-players, then Merdenne stiffened bolt upright, his pale face contorted in rage. "The king!" he shouted. "You've deceived me! Your accomplices–"

"Perhaps," said Ambrose mildly, "like your old friend Suleiman, you need to learn the value of pawns."

With a choked cry Merdenne leaped to his feet and dashed his fist to the centre of the chessboard, scattering the pieces in all directions. The diners at the nearest tables looked with shocked amazement at the reappearance of the two men. Merdenne's chair crashed backwards as he ran toward the door, knocking aside a waiter in his path.

Ambrose drained the last of the Latour from his glass before he stood, dropped several bills upon the table, and followed his double out of the restaurant.

But even as my hand reached for the knob, the door burst into flames. Arthur, Tafe and I drew back as one. The unnaturally bright, devouring heat of the blaze revealed its origin. "Too late!" I cried. "Merdenne is upon us!"

"The window," said Tafe. She let go of Arthur's arm, pushed the massive wing chair to the wall, lifted and toppled it through the glass in an explosion of glittering shards. I tugged loose one of the long drapes and knotted one end to a bent section of the now empty window frame.

As though from old habit, Arthur took command. "You go first," he said to me. "I'll need your assistance below."

Glad to be free of the stifling heat – the one entire end of the room was by now in flames – I stepped over the sill and rapidly lowered myself down the drape, then let go and fell the last few feet to the ground.

Arthur tossed the bundled Excalibur down to me, then half-clambered, half-slid down the drape. I caught and steadied him when he dropped the last distance. Tafe was only halfway down the drape's length when the knotted end burned free from its mooring. She fell heavily upon her back in a shower of sparks.

I helped her to her feet and she nodded to indicate that she was all right. The three of us hurried away from the inferno that Merdenne had made of his clinic in a vain attempt to trap us. Behind us, the walls of the building began to collapse, sending gouts of dizzying heat across the red-lit lawns.

"Here!" A voice shouted to us, carrying across the hubbub of the crowd that had gathered around the iron fence. I spotted Ambrose signalling and pointed him out to Arthur and Tafe. We turned our steps toward the spot and soon were separated from him by only the iron bars of the fence.

A group of good-hearted young Londoners, always ready to participate in any excitement, extended their hands through the bars like steps and helped us mount over the top railing. One by one we dropped down into their midst, then were collared into a group by Ambrose. As we began to work our way from the scene of the holocaust one of the cheerful mob shouted after me. "Hey, mate! You forgot your parcel!" The fellow tossed the bundled Excalibur over the heads of his comrades. I caught it, yelled a quick thanks to him, then hurried after the others.

5
Timely Strategies

This was the voice that had laid out the plans for the routing of the Saxon armies from the shores of Britain. In a rough castle, a fortress of hand-hewn stone and little light, this voice had given its orders and words of encouragement to the generals who served as comrades. And outside the walls this voice had roused the common fighting man, no less comrades for their lower rank; roused them to a fighting pitch that was like the true and murderous edge upon the inscribed blade that a scarred hand raised to glisten in the sun of those heroic Fifth Century days.

Now the voice was weaker, that of an old man, tired and weighed down with the cursed work done upon him by our adversary. In the ill-lit groggery near the river docks that Ambrose had led us to, as I sat and listened I tried to connect in my mind the old man Tafe and I had rescued with the powerful legends that were buried deep in the English soil and spirit. Was this really Arthur, the defender of Britain? Even now, after all I had seen and risked, doubt gnawed at my heart. How damnable was Merdenne's trickery that it could create such confusion! I drew my attention away from the darkness I carried inside and returned it to my comrades.

The pretence of "General Morsmere" had been dropped by all, in contrast to the pseudonym that still clung to him who would have been more rightfully called Merlin. Perhaps this indicated something about the essential character of the two figures – forthright warrior and devious magician.

Arthur lifted his beer with both frail hands wrapped about the mug and sipped at it. The recent exertions of his escape had left him considerably weaker than before – frighteningly so. He carefully set the beer back down on the table and continued speaking.

"This is how it came to pass," said Arthur. "One morning in my suite at the Savoy, I awoke and found myself dizzy and sweating as if frightened by my dreams. Upon rising from my bed I discovered that I was barely able to stand due to the trembling in my limbs. The weakness advanced throughout the day, accompanied by the most soul-numbing despair I had ever felt. Finally, in an attempt to restore my spirits and fight off the spell being laid against me, I opened the secret compartment in my military chest and took out my cherished Excalibur. The devastation of my hopes was total when I found it as you have seen, diminished in weight and the sacred inscription all but blotted out. I knew then that a dread evil was upon me. Merdenne arrived with the evening's darkness and I had no strength to resist him. Soon, thanks to his arrogant boasting, I was made aware of how my strength had been leeched away." He paused to moisten his throat again.

I glanced over at Ambrose with some unease. I had somehow expected that these two comrades of ages past, their lives so intertwined through the pages of English legend, would bear some special regard for each other and that these feelings would be apparent upon their being reunited once more. But I was unable to detect any such warmth between them. Was Ambrose so repelled by the change wrought upon his hapless friend to spurn him thus? How frail, I mused, are even the hearts of the immortals.

"It was done with that damnable device for Travelling through Time." Arthur's voice trembled with rage. "That Machine which the Morlocks stole from its murdered inventor – a sorry fool he! With the Time Machine Merdenne was able to travel to different points in history when Excalibur was not yet come into my hands. Through his own arts he located the sword at these different times and brought each one back to this time. Three times he did this, and thus diluted my powers."

My brow creased in puzzlement. "I'm not sure I understand," said I.

"The power that is embodied in Excalibur," said Ambrose calmly, "is a constant sum at all times. What Merdenne has accomplished is to bring four Excaliburs into being at one time. Thus, that power is now divided among the four swords – leaving Arthur similarly weakened." Oddly, he seemed not at all surprised by the revelation.

"But the inscription," said I. "What reason is there for the runes being almost obliterated?"

"Not obliterated," said Arthur. "But obscured. The meaning of the runes is scattered
among the four swords. If there was but one
Excalibur once more, then the inscription
could be read again."

"This seems hopeless, then." My glance
darted from one face to the other. "Even if
we could obtain the duplicate swords from
wherever Merdenne has hidden them, we
couldn't return them to their proper time
without the Time Machine which the Morlocks control. And how would it be possible
to wrest the device from them without first
restoring Excalibur and Arthur to their full
powers? Frankly, gentlemen, I can see no
way out of this deadly conundrum." The
logic of my arguments weighed on my soul.
Across the table the aged Arthur looked even
further sunk into bitter reflection.

Ambrose's fingers formed a cage in front
of his impassive face. "Well put, Hocker," said
he. "Indeed, there would be little chance of
rectifying the situation by merely reversing
the steps through which Merdenne created
all this mischief." His hands moved apart.
"But if another way could be found – dangerous yet possible – what say you to that?"

"The dangers would count as nothing," said Arthur fervently. "The possibility of achieving our goal would be all the calculation we needed."

An assenting nod from Ambrose. "I half-suspected, half knew of the multiple Excaliburs and the problem they pose us. But there are also factors in the situation that work to our advantage. To wit – the power that is presently divided among the four swords is in an unstable condition. It yearns to be gathered into one again. Wherever Merdenne has hidden them, they still seek to be united. If each one were to be located, seized from whoever has it, and brought against this one, their metals would meld into one sword, the inscription could be read again, and Excalibur's power would be as before. As would yours be as well, Arthur."

In my heart I damned myself for a doubt-ridden coward, but I spoke up again. "A dangerous undertaking, indeed," said I. "Now that we have liberated Arthur, as well as one of the Excaliburs, surely Merdenne has alerted those allies of his that hold the other swords. Their vigilance in guarding them will beat a ferocious pitch by now.'"

"I think not," said Ambrose. "The net of intrigue that binds Merdenne's agents to his service is weakened by corrosive suspicion on all sides. 'Thieves fall out,' as the old saw has it. If Merdenne were to reveal to his accomplices that we had wrested both Arthur and one of the Excaliburs from his grasp, his entire organisation might abandon its allegiance to him. No, I think Merdenne is forced to play a lone hand against us in this matter."

"But still," I said. "His cunning is now augmented with anger at having once been bested. He seems a more formidable opponent now than ever."

"Are you afraid of him, Hocker?" said Ambrose quietly.

My spine stiffened as his eyes, as well as Arthur's and Tafe's, focused upon me. "Of course I am," I replied with some heat. "If I'm to be the only prudent member of this little alliance, then so be it. I fancy I've acquitted myself as well as anyone here who considers himself absolutely fearless."

"Well spoken, that." said Arthur approvingly. "On the battlefield all hearts tremble, but the courageous hand lifts its weapon nonetheless. Here – I'll drink to that." He lifted his beer again, swaying a little as he did so. In his weakened state, the alcohol was making a strong impact on him.

"Actually, Hocker," said Ambrose, "you may not have to face Merdenne at all in order to acquire the other Excaliburs. I eliminated Merdenne from the scene before; I intend to do so again, leaving you a more open field in which to pursue your quest."

"But how?" He had already told us of the stratagem he had employed when Tafe and I had gone into the clinic. "Surely he would not be deceived like that again!"

"Though I always prefer deception to any other means, in this case it is not my plan," said Ambrose. "I intend to overpower Merdenne, to bring the full weight of my will and strength against him. As you say, there would be little hope of tricking him once more. I must follow a more dangerous course."

"How do you mean?"

He spread his pale hands out upon the table. "While you were in the clinic I had transposed Merdenne and myself into a future time when all London was empty of inhabitants. But I did not use my strength to attempt to hold Merdenne there. It would have been pointless, as his own strength would have been sufficient to elude my grasp and return to this Time. What I intend to do now is to forcibly transpose both Merdenne and myself into a point in Time so distant that neither one of us will be able to return by our own strength. We will be like those Arctic explorers who expend all their energy to push on toward the Pole, despite the knowledge that they lack the means of returning to warmth and comfort."

"But this is insane!" I cried. "Why, you'd be lost forever in some dismal period of the future, trapped in the world's wreckage with your bitterest enemy! And what hope could we who are left behind, have of locating the other Excaliburs and restoring the weapon to its proper state? I can't see how our chances are much improved with this proposed gambit of yours."

"Good old Hocker," said Ambrose, smiling, "with your quick, sceptical mind. To answer your first objection, I need not be trapped forever in the far future. All this mucking about with Time in which Merdenne and the Morlocks have engaged has frayed the fabric of the Cosmos to the ripping point. By restoring

Excalibur and Arthur's strength thereby, and then destroying that cursed Time Machine, you will restore the natural order of the Universe. The three Excaliburs that Merdenne snatched from their proper points in history will be automatically restored to those points, and I will be fetched back to this time once more. To carry my Arctic analogy a little further, I shall be like that explorer who has gone beyond the point of no return, only to be happily rescued and brought back to civilization by others."

"That is all well and good," said I, "but I fear you may yet find yourself stranded in Time's Arctic wastes. I still don't see how we, without your assistance, are to accomplish the task you have set us. Merdenne has no doubt hidden the swords in the farthest crannies of the Earth. And even if he hasn't revealed how he was tricked out of this one, his henchmen will still be on their guard against anyone who comes snooping after the swords."

"True enough." Ambrose remained unruffled in the face of my many protests. "It will take great courage and guile on the parts of all of you to accomplish what must be done. And failure is more likely than not, no matter how valiantly you struggle. But you won't be merely casting about in the dark for the scattered Excaliburs. As I said earlier, I have suspected for a little while the nature of Merdenne's plotting. Many persons of both high and low rank, odd and conventional positions, are in my employ, for one reason or another. Some of them value the same ideals as I do, others are a little more mercenary. They have all been enlisted to locate the hidden Excaliburs, and have met with some success. The swords are objects of such power, even in their weakened state, that they cannot long be hidden from eyes that know what to look for. These agents of mine will assist you in your task."

"How are we to contact them?" He drew a sealed envelope from his coat pocket and handed it across the table to me. "Here is the name and house number of the person whom I feel you should seek out first. It will soon be daylight. I would advise that the three of you retire to my residence and rest until this evening. Work of this kind, no matter how good its intentions, is best done under the cover of darkness, and you will need all your strength as well. In the meantime I will do that which I have set for myself. When you set out once more upon your errand, it will be in a world that holds no direct threat from Merdenne – or assistance from me."

Arthur tapped the side of his empty glass. "A course lined with pitfalls," he mused. "But I can see no other."

"We've done all right so far," said Tafe.

I struck the palm of my hand with the envelope Ambrose had given me, while refraining from voicing the doubts that crept upward along my spine. What good would it do to say that none of us – not even Ambrose – accurately knew the true nature of the accomplices of Merdenne from whom we had to wrest the several Excaliburs? Indeed, how trustworthy were the cohorts of Ambrose into whose hands we were entrusting our lives and mission? Misgivings darker than these, perhaps even unnameable, moved within me.

The sun's edge reddened the oily waters that lapped against the docks. I slipped the envelope that held the thread-end of our destiny into my breast pocket, just over my unquiet heart.

6
Seeking the Grand Tosh

A dark place that resisted the ascending light of morning; to this came a figure whose pale face and hands contrasted with his dark cloak. He pushed open the narrow, craze-hinged door and entered, leaving behind him the cramped street where the buildings leaned together to provide pools of shadow for the tattered forms of men and women, London's human refuse, that loitered at the base of the dark walls.

Candles guttered in the room, and shapes moved and watched beyond the yellow circles of light. Another face, so pale it seemed to shed its own ghastly radiance in the dark, turned away from its companion and up at the newcomer. "Dr. Ambrose." The voice was flat, unemotional. Only a narrowing of the eyes revealed the hate and loathing beneath.

"You left a chess game unfinished," said the newcomer. *"That's not like you, Merdenne."*

Pale also was the flesh of the other figure sitting at the table, but unhealthily so, like the belly of a rotting fish, damp and repellent to the imagined touch. A pair of blue glass lenses beneath the skull's fringe of fine white hair completed the face that followed the words of the two identical men.

"I have larger amusements to pursue," said Merdenne levelly. *"In fact, you have come upon me in the midst of discussing a point of strategy with my associate here."* The sick-looking face with the blue glasses nodded in hollow politeness. *"I fear I have no time for that smaller game."*

"No time?" Ambrose smiled. *"I think otherwise."* His hand darted forward and locked about the wrist of his double. The candles flicked out and the room was plunged into darkness. When the candle was lit again, the eyes behind the blue glasses saw a turned-over chair beside himself, and nothing else.

Ambrose painfully raised himself from the rubble-strewn ground. He touched his hand to the side of his face, looked and saw blood bright against his fingers. A ringing noise filled his ears.

A few yards away, Merdenne staggered to his feet. He shook his head, then gazed about him at the vista of ruined masonry, the crumbling fragments of a once great city. His eyes shifted focus for a few seconds, as if looking beyond the scene's material aspect.

"You fool!" He spun about on his heel and glared in fury at Ambrose. "You've trapped us here!"

Wearily, Ambrose sat upon the base of a shattered marble column. "We're not trapped," he said, gazing at grey clouds moving across a grey sky. "Just removed from the game for a little while. Let our pawns play out the moves we've arranged for them." He gestured at the scene around them. "This will pass, one way or another, when the struggle is decided." With a sharp-pointed stone he began to scratch at the dirt in front of his boots.

"What are you doing?" snapped Merdenne.

A cross-hatch of sixty-four squares showed in the dust. Ambrose began picking through the small stones around him, sorting out the darkest and the lightest and arranging them on the squares. "This will do for a rook," he said. "And here's your king… I believe you had just castled when we left off, though I'll let you take that move back, if you wish." He glanced up at Merdenne's scowling face. "Come, come." he chided. "We have a little time here. Can you think of a better way to pass it?"

Merdenne glared at him for a few more seconds, then without speaking sat down on the other side of the board inscribed in the dust.

I drew the envelope from my pocket and once more read Ambrose's message – *Tom Clagger can be trusted* – followed by a house number in Rosemary Lane. As the three of us – Arthur, Tafe and myself – had set out from Ambrose's lodgings just as dusk was setting upon the city and had spent some time searching fruitlessly for the mysterious Mr. Clagger's residence, it had now gotten quite dark. The mazy streets and alleys of this poor section of London, packed tight with the most wretched of the urban refuse, seemed even denser and less penetrable at night. I pocketed the envelope again and turned to my companions.

"I fear we have lost our way," said I. This, though we were not out of sight of some of the city's tallest landmarks! Such is the intricacy of these lesser explored urban parts. "Stay here and I shall seek directions." I crossed the narrow street and headed for a group of roughly clad men standing about the open door of an ale shop.

My undertaking was accompanied by a little trepidation, for in an area such as this the possibility of violence for the sake of robbery or even mere amusement is always something to be reckoned with. Our little expeditionary party had tried to dress as plainly as possible, but our great-cloaks simply by their cleanliness attracted the sinister attention of the loiterers on the street. But the urgency of our mission propelled me on toward the men who were even now scowling at my approach.

"Gentlemen," I said brazenly. "I'm looking for a Mr. Thomas Clagger. The price of a drink all around if you can direct me to him."

"Clagger? Clagger?" muttered one of the rag-tag band. "Don't know of no damn Clagger." His black-nailed hand strayed toward his pocket.

The others whispered among themselves until suddenly the face of one brightened. "Oh, you mean Rich Tom!" he called out. "Whyn't you say so?" His companions' faces took on less menacing expressions, as they now regarded me with some measure of respect. Clearly the name Clagger was one that carried a little weight in this district.

"Yes, that's the one," I said, hoping it really was. "Do you know him?"

"*Everyone* knows old Rich Tom. Why, he loaned me a crown when me wife was last confined and the nurses wouldn't give us the baby 'til we had paid a bit on the bill. Of course I know Rich Tom."

I signalled for Tafe and Arthur to come across the street and join me. "Can you take us to him?" I said, turning back to my new-found informant.

"I should think so," said he. "You're nowt but a few paces from his door where you're standing."

"Splendid." I distributed coins to the other men, who touched their caps and mumbled thanks, then stepped into the ale shop to test their value. "Can we hurry along? We've got some important business with Mr. Clagger."

"I'm on to you. Lord, I had no idea old Tom had such spiffy friends, but it makes as much sense as him having pots of money in the first place."

He escorted us to the opening of a court-yard that we had passed by several times earlier. "You probably missed it," said our guide, "cause the lane takes a little jog in right here. See? There's 'nother building around the corner." We followed him under the low arch. "That's his door right there."

In truth, we would have never found the well-hidden lodgings without the man's aid. I bestowed a coin of gratitude upon him and received a cheerful thanks.

Arthur looked about the cramped, crumbling courtyard with distaste as I rapped upon the door. The old king was most likely filled with bitter reflections about the degradation of his land. On the other side of the door I could hear shuffling footsteps. "Coming!" cried a man's voice from inside.

The door opened and a man's face peered out. He was not quite so old as Arthur, but well up in years, with a fringe of grey hair around the shining pink dome of his head. "Yes?" he inquired politely. "What is it?"

"Mr. Clagger?" I asked. "Tom Clagger?"

"That's right." He nodded happily, apparently quite pleased with being recognised.

"We're friends of Dr. Ambrose–"

"Ambrose!" he cried. "Well then, come in. Don't stand out there in that mucky courtyard." He ushered us into a small, well-lit parlour. The room was surprisingly clean and

tidy in a fussy bachelor's manner, in contrast
to the decaying neighbourhood surrounding
it. It was comfortably, if not expensively furnished, with a few framed sporting prints on
the walls above the time-worn chairs. An astonishing number of books lay about on the
tables and tops of cupboards, and arranged
in rows upon several sets of bookshelves.
Most of them showed the marks of having
been acquired at bargain prices-cracked or
mismatched bindings, water stains and the
like. There were no cheap novels among
them, but were all an impressively weighty
collection of philosophy, history and similar
topics. One that lay open on the arm of a
chair bore in the margins the pencil marks of
studious perusal.

"And how is Dr. Ambrose?" said our host,
gesturing for us to seat ourselves. His voice
bore just a trace of the uncultured accent of
the people in the nearby streets.

"I'm afraid he may be in some danger." I
sat down and studied the old man's expression. "There is, unfortunately, nothing we
can do to aid him at this time."

Clagger nodded thoughtfully. "Yes, I imagine such could very well be the case. Dr.

Ambrose is a man of powerful great learning, but– something more than that, too, as you might well know." His bright eyes peered sharply at me. "Mister… ahh…"

"Hocker," said I. "Edwin Hocker. And this is, ah, Mr. Tafe, and Brigadier-General Morsmere."

"Tut, tut," said Clagger reprovingly. "I'm at least a little ways into Ambrose's confidences. I'm honoured to have you in my home, my lord Arthur." He gravely inclined his head toward the king.

Arthur lifted his hand. "Please. No formalities. I hold a man of learning such as you as my equal"

"Yes, well, I'm not exactly what you'd call schooled, but as you can see I read a fair bit." Clagger waved a hand at his scattered library. "Quite famous for it in these parts, you know. Mr. Mayhew was the one who put me on to it."

"Mayhew?" said I. "Not Henry Mayhew, I take it?"

"Yes," said Clagger with obvious pride. "I've got a signed first edition of his *London Labour and the London Poor* somewhere around here. I was one of the people he interviewed in his research. Let's see – Lord, that was back in '49 or '50, I believe. How my heart broke when he died a few years back, for he'd become a true friend to me, and done me all the good in the world." He sniffed in sad remembrance of the great chronicler of London society.

My eye darted to an object I had seen when we had first entered the room, and had caused me a little wonder. Suspended on hooks over the fireplace was a pole some eight or nine feet in length with a curved hook on one end. His mention of Mayhew's book, which, like most educated Londoners, I knew to some degree, sparked my recognition of the singular object's function. "Why, you're a tosher!" I said. "A river-man, a sewer-hunter."

"Retired," he corrected. "Though I miss me old trade like anything on a clear morning, when the sun's just tinting the river's water by the outlet grates, and that stew of smells comes wafting out of the sewers at low tide isn't that fine, though." He pointed to the long object over the fireplace. "You see I've kept me old probing pole – many's the time it's served to save me very life, I tell you! – and I've got me old lanterns and leather aprons tucked about somewhere as well. Ah, what a grand life has a sewer-hunter, there's no doubt about that."

"I had no idea the calling enabled one to live as well as this," I said, gesturing about at his cozy residence.

"Ah, well, there's the kindness Mr. Mayhew did me. The calling *does* pay well, for all manner of valuable objects is lost into the sewers for the finding by those that know the ways. But most toshers spend their earnings on drinks and suchlike sprees as fast as they can get it. Mr. Mayhew, bless his memory, was the one who pointed out to me the folly of such rude practices, and how fast a little put by from one's findings would soon amount to a tidy sum. I followed his advice, though Lord! I got thirsty at times, and now the people in this district hereabouts call me 'Rich Tom,' though I'm prouder yet of the learning I've done meself in these years since I left the toshing trade. For it's that what prompted our mutual friend Dr. Ambrose to seek me out and enlist me in his projects."

My eyebrows raised in unbidden scepticism. "What exactly is it Ambrose consults you about?"

Our host lifted his chin with a measure of disdain. "Dr. Ambrose is a man of great knowledge, as you might expect, knowing who he really is, and he knows more about the London sewers than many of the toshers mucking about down there. But he doesn't know as much as I do."

"How much is there to know?" said I. "About sewers?"

"Sir, you reveal your ignorance. There's marvels beneath the street that would fair scatter the wits of the average fellow walking about on the pavement all unaware of what's below his feet. Places and ways *deeper and older than you can imagine*, my dear Mr. Hocker. And things, too – certain valuable things, if you catch me drift."

I did indeed. "So you know then what it is we are seeking?"

"I believe I do," said Clagger. "Though I can tell you the fetching of it will be no easy matter."

"The harder the task," said Arthur sternly, "the greater the glory." Tafe, seated away from him, rolled her eyes heavenward at his statement but said nothing.

I looked at the old king dubiously, then

turned back to Clagger. "There's little time." I said. "How soon can we start down there?"

"Me old pals have loaned me from their gear some of the stuff we'll need for our little expedition – lanterns and aprons, mostly. And I've got me old pole to help me test the way ahead of us. So I believe we can start at most any time you please."

"You'll guide us?"

"Of course," said Clagger. "Who else? And I can't bloody well give you a map, you know."

"I suppose not. Well, that's most kind of you then."

"I'll go fetch the gear." He got up and dis-appeared into the rear of his lodgings, coming back a few moments later with the traditional leather aprons used by sewer-hunters draped over his arm. From one hand dangled some battered tin lanterns with leather straps affixed. These, as I knew from my reading of Mayhew, were worn on the toshers' chests to light their way in the dark passageways under the London streets. Clag-ger deferentially handed one of the aprons to Arthur, but before his hand could grasp it the old king doubled over in a fit of cough-ing. As the choking and hacking died inside

him, he straightened up, pressing his handkerchief to his lips. Before he could put the
cloth away I was up from my chair and had
grabbed his thin wrist. He was able to put up
only the most feeble resistance as I turned his
hand over and revealed the spots of blood
upon the handkerchief.

We looked in grim silence at the blood,
then Clagger spoke. "You'll have to stay
here, my lord," he said. "You mustn't come
down into the sewers with us."

"Nonsense," said Arthur angrily. "I'm more
than capable." He jerked his hand free from
my grasp. "No," said Clagger, shaking his
head. "The cold and the damp and the noxious gasses make it no fit place for weak
lungs. It'd kill you for sure, and then where
would we all be?"

"He's right," said I. "Come, you're an old
soldier. Would you endanger the success of
a mission by sending along a man in your
condition?"

His red-flecked eyes glared fiercely at me
for a moment, then clouded with moisture
as he sank back into the chair. "Go on, then,"
he said, gesturing weakly at us. He looked
very old and shrunken now. "I'll... I'll keep

watch on the situation from up here. Yes, that's what I'll do. Stand guard."

We completed our preparations in silence, then left the old king there in the parlour, staring before him into his memories of ancient glories.

As we crossed the courtyard I drew Clagger toward me. "You see the urgency of our task," I whispered. "Not only his strength but his very life depends upon our finding the swords." He nodded and led us quickly on toward the river, his pole carried in his hand like some odd weapon of battle.

"Down here," said Clagger when we had reached a section of sagging wharves along the bank of the Thames. "There's a bit of a rope here you can lower yourself down on. I'm afraid those fancy boots of yours will be most ruined." He went before us to show the way down to the muck at the river's edge. The moon and stars glittered upon the oily, garbage- specked waters.

Tafe and I dropped down behind him. I reached over my shoulder and felt the bundled Excalibur where I had securely strapped it so that it would not impede my movements. We had decided to take it with us for whatever aid it might furnish us in locating its fraudulent brothers.

Splashing through the shin-deep, odorous mud, we made our way to one of the large iron gates of the sewer outlets. These were hinged so that they only opened outwards, to allow sewage to exit into the river yet prevent the water from backing up into the drains when the river was swelled by high tide.

Clagger got his hands under the edge, of the gate and lifted it far enough for Tafe and me to scramble into the circular opening beyond. He ducked himself under the gate, then let it fall behind him. With a resounding clang that echoed down the passageway, we were thus enclosed in the darkness of the London sewers.

A match sputtered into flame, then a shaft of light coursed in front of us from the lantern strapped to Clagger's chest. He helped us light our own lanterns. By their combined glow we could see quite well the drain's slime-encrusted walls leading on into blackness, and the torpid stream of filthy water that washed about our ankles. For several moments my breath, laden with the sewer's stagnant odours, caught gagging in my throat.

"It's a roughish smell at first," said Clagger. "But you'll get used to it. Just step along right behind me as we go and you'll be all right!"

His words proved true. After a few yards, both Tafe and I found our breaths coming easier to our lungs. The human body, prompted by the human will, is a marvel of accommodation to all manner of wretched conditions.

A scurry of tiny clawed feet sounded from somewhere beyond the reach of our lamps. Rats eyes, red in the lantern light, glared at our passage, then disappeared back into the crevices that served as their nests.

"Don't mind the little beasties," said Clagger. "They're not dangerous but when they're cornered. And then, Lord! How they'll fly at you! Some toshers think it's grand sport to hunt em, and probably think for all the world that they're just like the landed gentry on a fox hunt, but I've no mind for such foolishness."

Our little band was like an island of light moving through the dark world of the sewers. Our boots splashed in the shallow rivulets while our lanterns danced their beams over the walls covered with layer upon layer of ancient filth. More than once we had to squeeze past a throng of wet stalactites compounded from slow decades of flowing sewage. The damp air curled in our lungs.

My voice echoed from the curved walls as I broke the silence. "Clagger," I said, "where exactly are we headed down here? It strikes me that we've already gone some distance."

He turned around with one finger pressed to his lips. "Quiet," he whispered, then covered the aperture of his lantern and ordered Tafe and me to do the same. "There's a street grating up ahead," came his hushed voice.

I understood his meaning. Though sewer-hunting was a well-known profession among the lower classes, forming as it did something of an aristocracy among them, it was still technically illegal for people to enter the sewers for any reason other than the maintenance of them. If our lights and the noise of our passing caught the attention of a constable on the street overhead, our mission could be considerably interfered with. With Clagger to guide us there was little doubt that we would elude any efforts by the police to apprehend us, but the noise and general fuss of their search would frustrate the secretive nature of our quest.

Cautiously, we filed under the parallel slits of the street grating. I glanced up and saw the narrow sections of the night sky, the stars blotted out for a moment by someone's boot-soles as he crossed the street.

Once safely past, we uncovered our lanterns and proceeded. Our path curved downward and we were soon out of hailing distance of the surface world. At a wide point in the tunnel Clagger held up his hand for us to stop. "Quite a little stroll, eh?" he said, smiling. He took a small parcel from a pocket on the inside of his leather apron, un-wrapped it and divided hunks of stiff bread and cheese among us.

"So," said I, swallowing a dry mouthful, "where are we, Clagger? It all seems to go on forever down here."

"Patience, lad." The old tosher gestured with a hard crust. "We've gone quite a ways, there's no disputing that. But the hardest part is all ahead of us. Down we go now into the deepest and darkest parts of the city's sewers. And even beyond that…"

"What do you mean?"

"You'll see." Without further explanation he hoisted his probing pole and started in a sloshing trudge down the length of sewer tunnel. Tafe and I exchanged glances, then followed after.

We had gone what seemed like several more leagues when we halted at the edge of a crevice a couple of feet wide that ran alongside our path. "Look down here," said Clagger, bending over so that his lantern shone down into the hole.

From the extreme dampness of the crevice's walls I assumed that it was periodically flooded, perhaps by the high tide seeping in through an underground channel. At the bottom I could see a dully glinting mass of metal.

"See that?" Clagger's arm extended, indicating the metal amalgam. "Must be a hundred-weight or more of valuables – silver coins, brass nails and ship fittings, jewellery, what looks like a pewter christening mug… Lord, you'd be surprised at all the stuff what gets washed down here. It all gets rolled by the water into low places such as this, then becomes all stuck together by virtue of the constant passage of dirty water over it. A lump such as that is what we call a 'tosh' and other people call us 'toshers' because of 'em.

Many's the time when I was younger that I've found toshes big as me own head, taken 'em out under the bridge to bust 'em apart, and made more than five pounds from the coins alone. That one you see down there would be the making of someone's fortune, easy."

I pondered the lump below. "Why hasn't anyone taken it then?"

"Why, bless you, there's many that's tried! Old Rollicker Jim near cracked his skull open trying to rig a block and tackle to fetch it up, and only succeeded in bringing a piece of the sewer masonry down on his head. No, I fear that bloody tosh down there is too damn great and heavy to be gotten out. It'll sit there growing bigger by every dropped sovereign and penny-piece that comes to it until the end of time."

"It's growth may be over sooner than you think, then," said I. "We've no time to waste gawking at such things if we are to avert the disaster that faces us."

Clagger nodded, causing the beam of his lantern to shift back and forth across the metal lump. "You must know somewhat of where you're going, though, before you go rushing down there. I'm showing you this for reasons other than as a pretty sight on a Sunday promenade. Just where do you think you'll find that for which you're looking?"

"You mean that one of the Excaliburs created by Merdenne has been incorporated into a tosh like this?" I pointed to the glittering mass.

"Not just *a* tosh, if you please, but the greatest of all! The Grand Tosh!" The sewer walls rang with the sudden fervour in his voice. "Bigger nor houses, it is! Like a cold moon swimming up from the bottom of the sea!"

"You've seen such a thing?" said I. "How much farther is it?"

He sadly bowed his head. "Ah, well, if there was a tosher who'd seen the Grand Tosh, I'd be the one. I've been through every slimy foot of these sewers but never laid eyes on it. But it exists! God's truth, it does! I know it, and there – where else but there, in that hidden magnetic lode of all that's most precious and lost – there's the place you'll find the Excalibur that was thrown into these sewers."

By the time he had finished his impassioned outburst I was in despair. It appeared obvious that Ambrose's confidence in this man had been sadly misplaced, as he seemed now to be either senile or crazed from his long associations with the sewers. Our position looked desperate. What if the old sewerhunter collapsed, or refused to guide us farther, abandoning us to the dark, mazy pathways? Even if we were able once again to obtain the sunlight on our own, what purpose would it serve! We would be no closer to locating the precious sword that lay hidden somewhere in the depths. And all the while, time running out...

Clagger apparently perceived my anxious thoughts, for he straightened up from his stance over the crevice. "Have no fear," he said quietly. "I get a little emotional sometimes when I think about the mysteries of the sewers. But I assure you that I'm in complete control of my faculties. And while neither I nor any other tosher has ever seen the Grand Tosh, it *does* exist, all for the finding of that which you seek."

"But how can that be?" said I in perplexity. "If you've been all through the sewers and not seen it, then where is it? What folly are we pursuing down here?"

"Calm yourself, for God's sake." Clagger

raised his palm in a placating gesture. "It's not in the sewers, and that is God's truth. You must go *beyond* the sewers."

Again that hint that had baffled me before. Had the man's acquaintanceship with Ambrose engendered in him a taste for mystery-mongering? The problem with secret knowledge, I mused bitterly, is that no one ever wants to tell you any of it.

"See here," I exploded. "I'll be damned if I know what you're talking about. Beyond the sewers? What could possibly be beyond them except dead rock and earth?"

"Ah." Clagger tucked his pole under his arm in preparation for resuming progress. "Let's go along a little farther, and you'll see all soon enough."

I lagged a few yards behind him in order to pass a word in secret with Tafe. Although she was laconic at all times, she had not even spoken once since we had descended into the sewers, and I was curious to know her mind about our situation. Was it trust or suspicion behind her silence?

"What do you think?" I whispered to her. Ahead of us, Clagger led the way without turning around. "Our guide's inclined to be a touch peculiar at times. Is he on the up or not?"

"I don't know," said Tafe in a choked voice. "Maybe… maybe he is. I just don't know."

The strain in her voice startled me. I could see now that her lips were bloodless, clamped tight, and that her brow was furrowed with some anxiety greater than that troubling me. "What's wrong?" I asked in concern.

She shook her head. "Nothing. Just leave me alone."

"Are you sick? Do you want to stop and rest for a moment?"

"No," she snapped. "Just go on, will you? I'm all right." Suddenly her words exploded out of her. "My God, Hocker, don't you feel it? It's so far down here underneath the whole damned world, and so tight and dark. I can feel the walls pressing in on me and *I can't breathe*–" Her words choked off, and in her wide, staring eyes I could see the effort with which she forced control over herself.

Clagger had heard the outburst and now came back to study the situation. "Afraid of being so far underground, eh?" he said, then shook his head. "Should have left you topside along with the old king. You'll not be much good a-toshing down here, and we've got deeper to go yet."

"Then lead the way, damn you!" Her anger flared up. "I may not like this hole you find so bloody cheerful, but I'm not afraid of it. So go on – we've wasted enough time already listening to you babble about one damn thing or another."

With an air of dubious resignation he turned away and resumed his place at the head of our little procession. This time I stationed myself last as we went, to be sure Tafe didn't fall behind, paralyzed by her fear. My thoughts were grim as I plodded along behind the two. I had not realised until this time how much my own strength was dependent upon Tafe's. As a comrade-in-arms I had considered her first, and a woman second. Even now she bore up better under the burden of her unfortunate fear than most men who are similarly afflicted. Still, it left our expedition in a perilously weakened state.

We marched on through the twisting and turning passages, sometimes inching along on our hands and knees beneath some slimy mass, or wading thigh-deep in the turgid, odorous waters that ran beneath the great city. The scraping noises of claws and the bright red eyes of the sewer rats followed us from one niche in the walls to another.

Ahead, Clagger came to a halt and turned to face us. As we came up to him he began unstrapping the lantern from his chest. "Here's the place," he said, "that's been weighing on my heart since we started out. If we can't get past this point, all our efforts. have been in vain. Take a look ahead and see for yourself. Mind the edge there, it's a mite crumbly."

I stepped past him and found myself gazing out over what seemed a limitless underground ocean. The light from my lantern glittered across its still surface and was lost in the distance. The waters were dark and covered with an oily scum interrupted by faintly luminous patches like algae.

"It's not as wide as it is deep," said Clagger behind me. "But to be sure, it's some fathoms to the bottom."

"How are we to get across then?" Wading was obviously impossible here.

"Don't worry yourself. There's ways of doing that easy enough. First I must test the air, though."

He had fastened his lantern to the end of his long probing pole, and he now stepped beside me with it. Slowly he extended it over the dark waters. The flame bent with some subterranean draft but remained burning brightly.

"Ah, good," said Clagger. "There's air fit for us to breathe out there. Sometimes the putrefying masses that lodge in the depths rise up and break open, releasing such noxious vapours as would suffocate you like a giant candle snuffer. It's good luck for us that such is not the case at the moment." He pulled back the pole and removed the lantern from the end. "Go back down the tunnel a couple of yards," he said, restrapping the lantern to his chest, "and on the right you'll find a section of the brickwork that's been replaced with a dirty piece of canvas. Draw it aside and bring what you find out here."

The piece of canvas at the point of which he directed me was not merely dirty, but artfully daubed with plaster and mud so as to resemble a section of the sewer passage itself. Drawing the camouflage aside, I found in the hollowed-out niche behind a small boat complete to a pair of oars resting in the brass fittings on the sides.

Tafe and I dragged the boat to the edge of the dark underground sea where Clagger stood waiting for us. He placed a loving hand on the prow of the little craft, looking for all the world like some British admiral admiring his fleet's flagship. "It got washed into the sewers," he said, "when an India clipper sank at the docks during a storm. Somehow it drifted down here where I found good employment for it. I've kept it hidden so that less cautious folk might not try their luck on yon water and find it wanting."

The boat was soon lowered into the water and one by one we cautiously took our places in it. Clagger manned the oars and pushed us away from the ledge where we had been standing. With a few strokes it was out of sight and we were surrounded by the fetid ocean on all sides.

"What happens," I asked with a little trepidation "if one of the putrid masses you spoke of breaks open and releases its fatal gas while we're crossing this body of water?"

"In that case," said Clagger, laying his weight into the oars, "you hold your breath and I row like hell." His impassive face made no show if this was meant as humorous or not. "And now, sir," he continued, "I must caution you to hold your voice in check. For I know well that sounds travel over still water with great clarity, and it behooves us to go as subtly as possible."

"Why so? Who is there to hear us?"

He looked at me reproachfully. "Do I have to remind you who they are who've made their base here in the sewers?"

The Morlocks! My heart clenched with the remembrance of them. I had been blind to the true danger of the depths through which we were roaming, so intently had my mind been focused on the object to which our pursuit was aimed. Not only were we braving the natural hazards of the underground but perhaps the malevolent scrutiny of our most implacable enemies as well. Suddenly the darkness around us seemed alive with unseen but sensed eyes taking the measure of our very inch of progress and calculating the best moment for some treacherous blow.

I barely managed to suppress my growing apprehension, not eliminating it but only pushing it into a corner of my mind. No course but this one lay before us – but to pursue it called for as much bravery as we possessed. So we sailed on, so far beneath the streets I had once blithely walked upon, moving across an uncharted sea toward an unknown destination.

At the back of the little boat Tafe sat with her head hanging over the side. Her restrained fear of the close spaces served to make the placid rowing into a rough crossing for her. I said nothing, knowing that her pride would flare into anger at any word of sympathy. Instead I turned and looked ahead to our not yet visible landing.

Suddenly she spoke. "I think something's coming up," came her voice from behind us.

"Just keep your head over the side," I said, not turning around. "I can't imagine a more fitting place in which to dispose of your last meal."

"No, you fool," said Tafe impatiently. "I mean coming up *from down there*."

Clagger stopped rowing. The boat rocked from side to side as I vaulted to a place next to Tafe and peered down into the inky water. A row of some dozen or more yellow lights was visible through the scum at a considerable distance below us. As I watched the lights grew larger and more distinct, indicating their gradual rise toward the surface.

"What can it be?" I asked Clagger as he appeared at my elbow.

"It looks worse even than anything I'd feared we'd encounter," he said, staring anxiously down into the water. "I'd heard rumours from some of the other toshers but I'd dismissed them as nonsense and arrant fabrications."

"What? You know what it is?"

"Yes." His voice was sepulchral – with foreboding. "The Morlocks have apparently placed a vessel for travelling underwater here to assist them in preparing for their invasion of the surface world."

The row of lights was ascending much faster toward us. "A submarine?" I said incredulously. "Such as Jules Verne imagined? The Morlocks are operating a submarine here beneath the city of London?"

"Aye," said Clagger, "that's the look of it, but I fancy we'll know for sure in a matter of a few seconds."

"The oars!" I pushed him back toward his position at the middle of the boat. "Row away!"

"Where to?" said Clagger despairingly. "Have you no eyes? That thing, whatever it is, is coming up faster than we could possibly move in any direction."

His words proved true. No sooner had he spoken them than our small craft was borne up by a swell of water, spun about, then capsized. With a shriek of expelled steam the submarine broke the surface while a churning weight of dark, filthy water pulled at my limbs and plunged me far below.

I had had time to catch only a fraction of my breath in the few chaotic moments before my immersion. The feeling of suffocation was heightened by the complete darkness – the lamp strapped to my chest was of course extinguished – and the slimy, scum-filled water pressing upon me. Oily ropes of decaying matter clung to my limbs and entwined about me as I thrashed desperately in the wake of the emergent submarine. Clumps of foul debris plastered themselves to my face, while my body's desire to fill its aching lungs with air drove my mind to sheer animal panic. I clawed and kicked at the swirling dark mass about me, not knowing whether I was scrabbling toward the water's surface or deeper below. Once my hand struck that of another person – Tafe, probably – and our fingers clutched at each other for a second before the turbulent currents tore them apart again.

Just as my mouth was about to break open in a scream, not caring whether it might be choked off under fathoms of this lightless sea, my head lifted into the air above the surface. A draft of the thick, fetid atmosphere was as welcome to me as any clear spring breeze. I gasped, fell back under the surface, then kicked myself up again. Treading water, I looked about to see what I could of the disaster's aftermath.

There was not a sign observable in the total dark of my companions Tafe and Clagger. More disheartening, I could hear nothing of them struggling in the water or calling out to locate each other or myself. The sound of my own voice was weak and quickly swallowed up in the vast area. "Tafe!" I cried. "Clagger!"

No answer came. I was forced to assume that they were both drowned or swept away into some inaccessible part of the subterranean ocean beyond my powers of assistance.

The only thing offered to my senses at all was the sight of the submarine now wallowing several yards away from me. What the function of the row of lights along its top was I could not guess; perhaps a signalling device of some kind. By their general illumination I could make out the details of the underwater vessel that had come upon us. An ovoid tapering to a point at both ends, it had indeed the baroque appearance of an illustration to one of Jules Verne's fantastic romances. Odd fins and propulsive devices jutted out at angles from the bolt-studded flanks. It lay without further motion in the slowly subsiding waters.

As my strength was quickly being exhausted by the effort of staying afloat in the cold water burdened as I was with my sodden clothes and Excalibur strapped to my back, I resolved to approach the submarine. Perhaps the Morlocks who piloted it now felt that their mission was accomplished in the sinking of our little boat and our deaths from drowning thereby. I could perhaps grasp one of the submarine's protuberances unseen and regather my strength until the vessel submerged again. Or if it stayed on the surface I could remain with it until it reached its home port, wherever that may be.

Beyond that I had no plan, only the faintest spark of hope kept alive by the weight of the cloth-wrapped sword across my shoulders. However diminished its state, Excalibur still inspired in me a bit of the courage of our heroic British ancestors, as well as that of my lost comrades. I couldn't let myself sink with it into the foul depths of the underground sea until my last ounce of will was gone. As noiselessly as possible, not letting my hands breach the water's surface, I swam toward the submarine.

I soon had hold of one of the fins near the vessel's waterline and managed to pull myself into a sitting position upon it, with only the lower part of my legs left dangling in the water. Pressing myself close to the hull, I could hear various scraping and scurrying noises inside. I took them to be the footsteps of the Morlocks and the incessant throbbing and clanking of the vessel's engine. A great exhaust of steam bubbled into the water from an aperture a few yards away from me, and I was grateful for the warmth it gave me. I could feel blood and life returning to my chilled limbs. Although my plight had not been improved a whit, a tiny bit more hope filtered through my irrational heart.

The submarine still had not moved from the point where it had erupted upon my late

companions and myself. Was something
amiss inside? The hurried noises that came to
my ear through the metal seemed to grow
more frantic, with the footsteps pounding
back and forth from one end of the vessel to
the other. The engine alternately roared or
slowed almost to the point of stopping. Various propellers and fins dipped erratically in
and out of the water. The one I was perched
on tilted, but righted itself again before I could
slide off. From a distance the foundering submarine might have given the bizarre
impression of a giant sea turtle that had somehow lost the ability to coordinate its limbs.

My rapidly mounting suspicions about
what was going on inside the vessel forced
me now to revise my plans. I had saved myself from drowning by clinging to the
submarine, but neither my lost companions,
our overturned boat, nor any safe point to
which I could swim had since appeared. The
submarine gave no sign of progressing toward a landing, and was perhaps even in
danger of inadvertently sinking. As the various noises banged through the hull like
scrap metal in a dyspeptic mechanical oe-
sophagus, I pondered my chances.

Finally, more from a lack of better ideas than anything else, I began to inch my way higher on the vessel. I had the vague notion that I could perhaps find a hatch or vent through which I could better discover the state of affairs inside. To what purpose I could put such knowledge I had no idea.

Using the various fins and propeller shafts for handles, I dragged myself to a point where I was lying prone upon the curved top surface, stretched between two of the glowing lights we had first spotted underwater. My calculations were at least partly correct. Through a tiny ventilator shaft with a cover that apparently closed with submersion in the water, I could hear distinctly the voices of the Morlocks inside. Their harsh gabbling was raised in argument – that much was clear, though I could understand none of the words. Volleys of scorn, accusation, contempt and other vocal passions sounded below me.

Had a mutiny split their ranks? I wondered. Their ferocious debate gave no sign of lessening, and the submarine's erratic twitches, meanwhile, continued. Perhaps, I hoped wildly, a fight would break out among them leading to a general slaughter, and I would be left the sole living tenant of the submarine. I dismissed the notion; it was too much to wish for.

So intent was I upon my eavesdropping that I almost didn't hear the slow opening of a hatchway behind me. Only when the circular metal door was thrown back upon its rasping hinges did I turn my head and see a pair of Morlocks come boiling out of the submarine's interior, their dead-white hands outstretched for me.

I leapt to my feet as they came scrambling across the hull toward me. Backing away as fast as I could upon the slippery metal, I interposed a large upright stanchion between myself and them. This brought me only a few second's grace, as I could see several more of their kind emerging from the open hatchway to join in the chase.

Hastily I decided to give up my position on the submarine. With no time to order my thoughts, I instinctively resolved that it would be better to swim or drown in the cold water than to be captured by the Morlocks and put to whatever filthy uses they could devise.

The curve of the submarine's hull was too great for me to clear if I tried to dive directly from it into the water. I quickly dropped to my stomach again and half-slid, half climbed down to the vessel's waterline. The hand of one of the Morlocks caught me by the collar of my jacket and stopped me from slipping into the water. I let go of the fin I was using as a handhold, grabbed his arm, then pulled him off his feet and in an arc over my head. I heard him collide with a spinning propeller, shriek as its blades tore at his flesh, then fall into the water.

More hands clutched at me from above, but I had slid far enough down the hull to be out of their easy grasp. A heavy iron bar whirred down toward my head. I twisted to one side and the weapon struck the submarine's metal flank with a dull clang. I turned my head away from my pursuers in order to spot the next foothold I needed for my descent.

A loop of rope fell across my throat and tightened in back of my neck. My hands flew to the noose in which one of the Morlocks had caught me, but it was already pressing into my flesh and cutting off my breath. I felt myself jerked back up the side of the submarine by the rope while the dimly lit waters grew even darker.

Hands I could no longer see grappled at me. I struck back in all directions, landing a few blows on their soft, clammy faces, until my weakened arms were at last forced behind me and tied with another section of rope. Gasping for air, with a spinning world roaring dizzily through my head, I felt myself dragged toward the submarine's hatchway.

7

Problems of Navigation

I came to, trussed up and tossed against a bulkhead. I had never gone completely unconscious, but the choking and rough handling from the Morlocks had quite dazed me. My body, if not all of my mind, remembered clearly being dropped down the hatchway ladder like a sack of potatoes. And then there had been much shouting and arguing in the Morlocks' harsh tongue, and their pale, brutish faces swimming through the black veil of blood that covered my eyes, peering at me, then disappearing again.

My head cleared a bit more as I shook it. Upon investigation I found that my back was to a large brass pipe that ran up to the submarine's curved roof, and that my hands were knotted securely behind me on the

other side of the pipe. I experienced a brief
flash of panic when I realised that the sword
Excalibur was no longer strapped to my
back. My fears were quickly assuaged, however, when I glanced about and saw the
cloth-wrapped bundle, now sodden and
stained from the underground ocean, lying
a few feet away from me. The Morlocks had
not troubled themselves to unwrap it to see
what was inside.

The compartment in which I lay bound appeared to be the submarine's engine room.
Several yards away was a maze of pipes and
shafts, some covered with black grease, some
glowing red with heat, all twisting and intertwined about the great cylindrical mass of the
main boiler, from whose various gauges and
apertures gouts of steam hissed out as though
a covey of dragons had housed themselves in
it. Long brass rods for the purpose of controlling the engine's valves and other parts were
connected to the machinery by intricate sys-
tems of gears and chains, then led through
metal rings on the ceiling toward the other
end of the vessel.

At one time the submarine must have been
a marvel of engineering such as no nation on

the Earth's surface had ever possessed. Now, though, it was in a sorry state of neglect and abuse. The metal, where not covered with grease and dirt was all pitted and corroded. Several of the brass controlling rods were bent or stuck tight in the rusted metal rings that held them. The glass faces of the gauges on the engine were shattered or smeared over with grease, and the escaping steam from the engine fully indicated its leaky condition.

From all this I surmised that the submarine was not originally the property of the Morlocks, that they had in fact come into possession of it by foul means, and were using it for their base purposes without thought of properly caring for it. Like most plunderers they took a general delight in seeing the goods of others degraded and trampled beneath their muddy boots.

To whom then had the submarine belonged? In the cunning of its mechanical design it was far advanced of anything produced above ground, yet as I studied it I noticed some curious anomalies. Various panels and corners of the machinery were decorated with engraved lines that formed the complex curved patterns employed by

the ancient Celtic artisans of the British Isles'
distant past! I had studied ancient artefacts,
and considered myself something of an am-
ateur archaeologist, and I easily recognised
the intricate knot motifs and stylised designs
– yet here they were not applied to brooches
and dagger handles, but to a complicated
technological device.

A puzzle, indeed. Surely no ancient
Britons had ever had the knowledge or resources to build such a craft as this
submarine. Who then had?

My mind's probing of this knot was interrupted by the sound of the Morlocks' voices.
I heard them coming toward the chamber
where I was bound, still arguing volubly
among themselves. A group of them burst
through the engine room's doorway and surrounded me where I sat tied to the brass pole.

I was a good deal more gently treated by
them this time. One of them pulled me to my
feet, untied my hands, pushed me away from
the pole, then retied the knot behind me
again. Their jabbering, excited debate continued as they pushed me through the door.

This was my first chance for a close observation of the enemies of Mankind. The pale,

clammy skin of their faces and hands was even more loathsome up close than at a distance, and the white flaxen hair that ran from their brows down along their necks was an additional sepulchral note. One was reminded unnervingly of those stillborn foetuses kept in jars of spirits at medical colleges, with their dead, translucent flesh.

My captors were dressed in dark brown military uniforms with various symbols of rank sewn to their sleeves. Any semblance of command or respect for their officers was lost, though, as they shouted and struck each other on the chest and shoulders to reinforce their point with a mutual barbarity. Round lenses of dark blue glass covered their eyes, and if these glasses were jostled from their position on anyone Morlock's face, his great goggling eyes screwed up tight with pain from the submarine's illumination until they were once again covered.

Through the submarine's central corridor they hurried me forward until we arrived at the pilot chamber where all the overhead brass control rods terminated. Here they were connected to banks of levers and knobbed wheels that served to adjust the various workings of the engine. Other groups of brass rods ran off in other directions. These I assumed were to control the submarine's fins and other steering devices. A system of lenses and mirrors provided the means of observing what lay outside the hull from many different angles – this, I surmised, was how the Morlocks had detected me clinging to the exterior of their craft.

But the most astonishing thing contained in the pilot room was not part of the vessel's equipment at all. Slumped down at the base of the banks of controls was a crumpled, motionless body. Upon my entrance under guard into the chamber I at first took the figure to be a heap of discarded laundry, then a sleeping, drunk, or otherwise insensible Morlock. As my accompanying troop brought me near to it, I saw the upturned face and realised that it was in fact a dead human being.

The cause of the man's demise was quickly apparent. He had been shackled by one ankle to a heavy metal chain that was in turn fastened to the front of the controls. Through long, diligent effort the man had evidently managed to sharpen a link of the chain against the rough textured floor, until the link had acquired a cutting edge equal to that of a knife. He had then employed it on his wrists. The floor around the corpse was stained with his dried blood.

Another mystery – whence had come this human pilot who had preferred death to the continued guidance of the Morlocks' submarine? I had little time to ponder the question, though, as they roughly pushed me forward to the post where the corpse lay. With a maximum amount of jostling and arguing the Morlocks proceeded to unlock the metal circlet around the corpse's ankle, and transfer it to my leg.

So careless were they in not dragging away the body of their former pilot, and so fractious in their conduct toward each other, stopping every few seconds in the re-shackling process in order to hurl imprecations and minor blows against each other, that when they were done all they had managed to accomplish was to place the shackle back upon the dead man's ankle, believing it to be mine. Their handicapped eyesight prevented them from noticing their error, and naturally I did nothing to reveal the condition to them, even arranging my position next to the body so as to conceal the true state. Whatever the ensuing events were to be, I preferred to face them in as unhindered a fashion as possible.

The arguing and general disorder among my captors lessened, and a pair of the Morlocks whom I took to be the highest in rank, due to the abundant decorations and insignia upon their uniforms, fumed their vocalising to me. The whole race of them being of an excitable and unrestrained nature, similar to the natives of Southern Europe in contrast to the more restrained British, the two Morlock officers were so given to gestures of the hand and facial motions that I could nearly divine their meaning from pantomime alone. Beyond this, however, I found myself starting to be able to understand fragments of their speech. The language seemed to be a grossly degenerated sort of pidgin German with infusions of exotic Slav and Oriental tongues with which I was for the most part unfamiliar, all spoken with slobbering labial explosives and harsh guttural stops that sounded like the clearing of mucus from their throats. All in all, a barbaric mode of speech that well fit their bestial nature. Most of it was beyond my comprehension, but l was able to pick up enough to catch their meaning.

The gist of their communication was that the previous pilot had killed himself, as I readily could see, and they were unable to guide their submarine themselves. My suspicions about their having illicitly appropriated the vessel were thus borne out. All of the controls were too small and delicate in their adjustment for their thick fingers to make use of.

Pilotless, they had had the good fortune to capture me. Now they intended to impress me into the empty position, apparently under the belief that I was of the same nature of person as the deceased pilot and not suspecting my true origin from the surface of the Earth. I was unable to tell from their discourse whether their raising of the submarine and capsizing of the little boat had been a fortunate – for them – accident, or a deliberate action clumsily executed. Of the submarine's true history, or that of its late pilot, I was able to learn nothing.

I quickly decided not to attempt to communicate to my captors that I knew not a whit of how to operate the strange vessel. Given the Morlocks' cruel natures, if I had succeeded in telling them this they would most likely have jettisoned me out into the cold underground ocean to drown. No, my one tactical point against their superior numbers and position was that I held no illusions about them while they were severely mistaken about me.

To gain time in which to formulate a strategy, I pantomimed with much holding of my hands over my ears and other gestures that I could not proceed with the piloting of the submarine unless my captors backed away and gave me a little peace and breathing room. So eager were they to be rescued from their hapless floating in the middle of the underground sea that they quickly acquiesced. With a flurry of shouting at each other like a kennel of dogs in an uproar, and mutually exchanged blows, they backed away from me and the banks of controls.

I turned my attention to the rows of wheels, knobs and levers laid out before me, trying to restrain my mind's apprehension about the situation I was in. Adrift in an underground ocean, surrounded by a horde of

K W JETER   185

the cruellest enemies of mankind, with the
dead body near of one who had killed himself
rather than serve them, and now attempting
to pilot a bizarre submarine, the like of which
I had never seen – and to what destination?
If by some chance I succeeded in steering the
vessel to whatever harbour the Morlocks de-
sired, what would they do with me then? Kill
me outright, or leave me to the same self-ad-
ministered fate as the poor soul lying at my
feet? More likely I would only manage to ex-
pose my ignorance about the submarine and
its controls – how long would it be before the
sharply watching Morlocks perceived it?
Whatever glimmer of hope had led me this
far into such a situation now seemed, the
more I reflected upon it, utterly extinguished.
It was with a dark and leaden heart that I
pulled my thoughts from my predicament
and studied the submarine's controls.

The curious features I had noticed in the
engine room were borne out on the controls
as well. The repeated intricate designs of ancient Britain decorated the corners and
spaces of the panels, and the spokes of the
several wheels were formed into intertwined
snake shapes. As I looked closer at the

gauges and dials I saw that their calibrations were marked off in runic letters and figures. A certain sadness crept into me at the thought that I would most likely be dead before I ever came to the bottom of this mystery surrounding the vessel's origin – a marvel of advanced technology apparently crafted by ancient Britons.

I could hear the Morlocks growing somewhat restless behind me, so I resolved to make some small experiments with the controls, hoping that I could learn a rough mastery over the vessel from whatever results ensued.

One of the large wheels seemed a good place to begin. I gave the most central of them a quarter turn, and one of the brass rods overhead moved correspondingly. Nothing else happened. Perhaps, I reasoned, the adjustment had been too slight to effect any change upon the submarine. I gave the wheel a full turn and was nearly toppled from my feet as the submarine tilted abruptly to one side. Only by retaining my grasp upon the wheel did I remain upright.

The general hubbub from the Morlocks became more threatening as they disentangled themselves from each other. I hastily turned the wheel back to its original position and the submarine slowly righted itself. At this rate, my value to the Morlocks as a pilot wouldn't last much longer. What I could understand of their comments on my performance was taking on a decidedly hostile tone.

My further attempts with the controls – turning wheels, pulling levers and the like in a frenzy of activity – met with little or confusing results. Either nothing happened when I manipulated one of the controls, or the submarine pitched and swayed in the water to no purpose. Either the Morlocks' neglect of the vessel's mechanisms had rendered most of them useless, or the mysterious corpse at my feet had somehow before his death managed to sabotage the workings.

During all this time I was aware of the Morlocks' patience with me running out. At any moment they might suspect the false colours under which I was running, and fall upon me. Not daring a glance behind me at the grimly muttering chorus, I reached up and pulled the first of an untried series of levers.

Just as with all the others, I thought dis-
gustedly when no apparent result could be
perceived. I was about to try something else
when I noticed a finger of water inching
across the floor toward my feet. The water
was emerging from a doorway that opened
onto a corridor running toward the front of
the submarine. Through the Morlocks' continuous garbled chattering, I could hear the
distantly gurgling noise of water splashing
against metal.

An odd situation. Apparently the lever
opened or shut some aperture that admitted
the surrounding water directly into the submarine's interior. Perhaps the tanks that
controlled the submarine's rising or descend-
ing by taking in or spewing out water had
become disordered to allow this. I was about
to return the lever to its original position and
shut off the water's inflow when, in a flash,
my mind leapt to the strategic possibilities
contained in the situation. With a decisive
motion I pulled the lever down all the way,
then did likewise with the similar levers
arranged next to it.

This time the results were satisfyingly immediate. Splashing and gurgling sounds

echoed from every angle of the submarine. The acrid scent of the sewage-tainted ocean clogged the air as a low wave of dark water pulsed through the open doorways into the pilot room.

No sooner had the noisome flood washed across the feet of the Morlocks than the high-ranking pair, medals and insignia jangling, came rushing up behind me. Both jabbered ferociously at me while one gripped my shoulder in his clammy white hand, spun me around and gestured angrily at the rising water, now past our ankles as it rose.

With an expression of bewilderment and frantic movements, I made a great show of expressing an inability to stem the flood. I beat futilely upon the ranks of controls, wrung my hands piteously and tore at my hair, all while the dark water crept steadily upwards. At last the Morlocks comprehended the message I was pantomiming. Most of my adjustments to the controls had been hidden from them by my body, so they had no idea of what particular lever or wheel was responsible for the incoming water.

If my captors had been garrulous before, they were positively babbling now. As the water rose over our shins the whole troop of them engaged in a vocal uproar like the baying of panic-stricken animals. At some point in the general bedlam the consensus was apparently reached among them to abandon the submarine rather than to go down with it. With hurried rushing back and forth, colliding with each other, shouting dreadful gibberish imprecations at each knocking of heads as they splashed backwards into the rising water they sought to implement their plan of escape.

From some locker in the rear of the submarine a pair of small collapsible boats and a number of leather vests with large, balloon-like air bladders sewn into them were produced. The Morlocks scrambled for the latter, two or more often tugging at one vest until one managed to wrest it from his fellows, though at last all the brutes had managed to don them.

The collapsible boats were opened and set up, and rushed by all hands toward the ladder that led to an overhead hatchway. All the Morlocks scrabbled to be nearest the boats, as there was quite obviously not enough spaces in them for all, and those left over would have to take their chances on bobbing in the underground ocean supported solely by their air-filled vests. After much futile hoisting, straining, and dropping back into the water, it was discovered that the boats were too large when opened up to go through the hatchway. With the boats folded back into their original shape they tried again. This time they succeeded in pushing them up through the exit, and clambered after as packed together as a swarm of bees. I shouted after the last ones and rattled the chain connected to the banks of the submarine's controls. Through piteous gestures and sounds I implored them to release me. The last pair of Morlocks laughed scornfully at me and climbed after their fellows, leaving me to a death by drowning. Most likely they felt I deserved it due to my poor piloting of the submarine.

As soon as they had all vanished from the chamber, I stepped away from the controls and the corpse that the Morlocks had mistakenly re-shackled to the apparatus. For a second I let my expression dissolve into a frankly gloating smile of self-approval.

Thus far my hastily conceived plan had

worked better than I could have hoped.
Above my head, through the open hatchway,
I could hear the Morlocks launching their
two little boats into the underground ocean,
the clamour of their struggle to gain places in
the boats, and the splashing about of those
who had already chosen or been forced to
land in the water itself. I had been left sole
master of the submarine. Though partially
flooded, it remained buoyant enough to remain floating. Surely I could find means of
remedying enough of its malfunctions in
order for it to convey me to some safe landing. What I would do from that point on I left
for the future and its chances to decide. I
turned back to the controls in order to halt
the inflowing water. Sharp, percussive noises
that I couldn't quite identify sounded from
outside the vessel, but I had no time to puzzle
over them.

The levers were beyond my power to
move. I tugged in growing desperation at
them, losing my footing in the now waist-
high water and hampered by the hobbled
corpse washing against me in a grisly manner, but the controls remained stuck in
their new positions. Either the controls or

the mechanisms they operated had been
frozen in place by the water pouring into
the submarine.

My mind racing like a rat caught in a rain
barrel, I saw that I too would have to follow
the Morlocks and abandon the vessel. Perhaps I could yet swim to safety. I slogged
through the chill, fetid water that was flood-
ing the chamber and was halfway up the
ladder that led to the open hatchway when I
realised that the cloth-wrapped Excalibur
was still somewhere in the engine room
where I had originally been bound. If the
precious weapon sank with the submarine to
the well-nigh bottomless depths of this dark
ocean, then all would be lost. There would
be no point in my even escaping with my
life, except to share in my fellow Mankind's
eventual doom.

I lowered myself back into the water and
half-swam through it toward the opening of
the corridor that ran back to the engine
room. The current pressing against my chest
made my progress maddeningly slow. I was
only a matter of several yards down the
passageway when the submarine's interior
went pitch dark, and the vessel itself began

to tilt. The back section, made heavier by the weight of the engine, was pulling the submarine into a vertical position as it sank. How would I manage to find Excalibur in an unlit and submerged space filled with strange machinery? By now the brass control rods were close enough overhead for me to use in pulling myself down the corridor. Every panicking nerve in my body pulled me the other way, back toward air and light. I felt the passage tighten about me as I descended into its stifling depths.

The way seemed endless and I began to doubt my memory of the passage's length. The water at last reached the top of the downward sloping space, and I was forced to take a deep breath and pull myself under with one hand on the brass rods. With my other hand I found the top of the engine room's doorway a yard or so farther along the submerged corridor. I let go of the reds and swam down into the lightless chamber.

The water fought against my every motion as I fumbled about blindly in it. My lungs were already aching when my hands at last touched upon the pole to which I had first found myself tied. I drew myself along its length to the now sharply tilting floor and felt about for the cloth bundle that contained Excalibur. I found nothing – the sword had probably slid to the deepest part of the room.

The blood was roaring in my ears by this time and my lungs hammered with every pulse for air. A deeper blackness than the one surrounding me was welling up behind my eyes. I could search for the sword no longer. Pushing myself away from the floor, I swam toward the room's doorway.

The nightmare of cold and suffocation had no end – I had lost the doorway. An infinity of dark water without escape stretched in all directions from my blindly groping hands. Like a drowned cat I floated upwards, willless and limp.

My face broke into air and hungrily, automatically, my burning lungs drew it in. Consciousness rose from the near corpse of my brain and I lifted my hand to discover the nature of this miracle. Apparently a pocket of air had been caught in one of the room's corners and I had drifted into it.

I filled my lungs several times over and dived back under the water. This time I swam as far as I could, seeking out the room's lowest point. Wedged between a corner of the engine and a bulkhead I found the bundle and felt Excalibur's length inside of it. With the replenished air starting to burn in my lungs, I kicked myself up through the water and by God's grace found the doorway immediately to hand. An agonizingly long way through the corridor, I at last broke through to the not yet submerged portion of the submarine. The foul air of the sewers that I breathed in seemed to me like the freshest wind that had ever blown.

The overpowering fear of drowning was gone, but I still had to escape the sinking vessel itself. I clutched Excalibur to my chest and swam to the side of the unlit space I was in. I fumbled my way along the bulkhead until I came to a metal ladder. Praying that it led to an exit, I clambered up.

My luck still held. I found myself on the sloping topside of the vessel. For a moment my brain, exhausted by my struggling, doubted what my eyes revealed.

The surface of the underground ocean was lit up by a score of torch-bearing boats forming a large ring about the submarine. The boats were slowly drawing nearer and closing the gaps between each other. I recognised now that sound I had been unable to identify from inside the submarine. It was the rattle of massed gunfire. By the flickering illumination of their torches I could see that the occupants of the boats were men such as I. In the prow of each boat one man stood with a rifle and levelled it repeatedly at his targets in the water. The shots echoed hollowly against the distant confines of the sewers.

Looking closer about the submarine I now saw the Morlocks' two collapsible boats lying overturned in the water. The figures of the Morlocks themselves were scattered about, most floating face downward, seeping red into the dark water. A few were still thrashing about, trying to escape the hail of gunfire that pocked the water around them. The softer noise of metal entering flesh accompanied the passing over of each of the swimming Morlocks to join his brothers in death.

Who were these marksmen in the boats? And from where had they come to be down here? As baffling as these mysteries were to me, I was overjoyed to see them, if only to glimpse once more the familiar outlines of human faces. So intent was I upon watching their encircling hunt of the remaining Morlocks that I was reminded of the submarine's sinking only when the water washed across my feet. I hurriedly scrambled to the small section of the vessel that was not yet under the surface of the water and began shouting and beating on the metal of the fin to which I held in order to attract the attention of the men in the boats.

A bullet clanged upon the fin just over my head to show that I had indeed caught one of their number's eye. More shots followed, ringing upon the submarine's hull around me. They had mistaken me for one of the Morlocks, I realised with a dismayed horror. The noise of their rifle fire drowned out my calls to them. Their torches were still too far away to illumine me as a target, but the accuracy of their shots would soon improve as they rowed closer.

The boats were approaching from all directions, so that there was no safety on either side of the large fin upon the base of which I huddled. A dark coldness washed against me as this last section of the hull slid under the water. If I clung to the submarine I would drown – if I let go and swam, I would be shot by the hunters in the boats.

My mind froze between these two grisly choices, but my body clung with animal tenacity to life. The water came across my chest where I had thrust Excalibur inside my shirt. My fingers locked with death-like rigidity to the edge of the fin while my lungs sucked in what would be my life's last few breaths.

The fastest of the boats came gliding to within a yard of my head as I held it above the water's chill surface. By the light of their torches I saw the gleaming metal barrel of the rifle point down toward me. *So it's death by bullet*, I thought with unnatural lucidity and closed my eyes as I heard the click of the hammer pulled back.

"Wait! For God's sake, don't shoot!"

I heard the voice crying and thought I had gone mad, for it was Tafe's voice. I opened my eyes and saw her in the boat's prow, pushing aside the man with the rifle and reaching for me, just as the submarine lurched beneath me and sank, pulling me

with it away from the light and down into
the dark and unrelenting cold.

8

The Lost Coin World

"Well, Hocker, we all thought we'd just about lost you that time. How do you feel?"

My eyes opened wide, letting light and consciousness drain away the last clinging dregs of sleep. For some reason I had been dreaming about a chess game played in a vista of ruins... No matter. The fantasy ebbed, replaced by the even more bizarre reality I was in. I focused on Clagger's kind, ruddy face and nodded. "I'm doing all right," I said, and raised myself on my elbows. I was lying in the middle of a large bed. "Where's Tafe?"

"Somewhere about here," said Clagger, "getting dry. Or as dry as one can in these clammy regions. You were well under, you know, when Tafe jumped in to fetch you out.

Said she had the damnedest time prying your fingers loose from that thing."

The memory of the submarine and the dark, enclosing water came spilling back into my mind. So I had been spared that death… for what? Another even worse? An overwhelming fatigue swept through my body and my thoughts were paralysed with a deep, foreboding dread of the future and all it might hold. Hope was born in the sunlight upon the Earth's surface; down here in the gloomy bowels of rock and muck it died.

My dismal meditation was broken by Clagger. "Come on, then," he said. "Put on your clothes and let's be about our business. I fancy there's quite a few questions you'd like to ask. To throw a little light in the darkness, that is to say. What? None at all?" He tossed my clothes – dried and mended by some unknown agency – across the foot of the bed.

"Just wait a few seconds," I snapped somewhat irritably. "I'll have questions enough for you, though what bloody good the information will do is beyond me at the moment."

While I dressed I cast an ill-tempered eye over this chamber in which I found myself. It held the aspect of what can only be described as decayed opulence. The bed itself where I had lain recovering a measure of my strength was little more than a sagging heap of brocades and other fancy materials, now tattered and soiled with countless years of use and neglect. The silk covering of the pillows, made thin with wear, was all split and water-stained. Over sections of the dark stone walls were hung heavy embroidered draperies, but these too were rotted away by Time. Their torn centres sagged to the floor like the slack skin of old men.

Over everything was the inescapable feel of dampness and rot, as though the vapours of the sewers had penetrated through every atom of things down here. My own skin now felt like that, undergoing a sewer-change down into my bones. I shuddered involuntarily as I drew my clothes, really only relatively dry, over my limbs. What awful metamorphosis would overtake me if I didn't soon return to the surface world's light?

Clagger was still waiting for me. "What place is this?" I said. "I take it that this is the region to which you meant to guide us, as you show little anxiety about being here." For the moment I laid aside the question of how he and Tafe had escaped drowning in the underground ocean. That was simply another piece of my ignorance to be filled in.

"This is it indeed." said Clagger, nodding in vigorous assent. "And not many a tosher could have found it, either. For of all of them that have heard of it, only a few would know the way."

"I'm well convinced of your knowledge." The old sewer hunter's boasting was becoming tiresome to me. "But still… what is this place?" The old man's grey eyebrows arched with the importance of the revelation. "None other," he intoned, "than that known as the Lost Coin World."

"Never heard of it."

"Your ignorance is a pity, then, and none the less either for being shared by all those who have never trod the sewers' paths. Even the greenest boy fumbling under the street gratings for a dropped shilling has heard of this place."

I drew on my boots and stood up. The damp mound of my bed sighed like a gratefully released animal. "Since a certain evening some time ago," I said, "when I first talked with our mutual friend Dr. Ambrose, the appalling extent of my ignorance has regularly been revealed to me. The only other fact with which I've become as well acquainted is the way that anyone who knows anything will go to any length to spin it out into a mystery."

"Aye, you're right enough about that." He absorbed the comment without any recognition that it could have been directed at him. "It took a fair amount of persistence, I can tell you, to get these people down here to tell me something of themselves. I wasn't just asking out of idle curiosity, either, mind you. It was all for the highest of scientific and historical purposes that I wanted to know."

"I'm sure of it. What were the results of your, ah, investigating?"

"Ah, Mr. Hocker, there's as much to tell as would make a man thirsty to relate it all, even in a damp set of environs such as this. So wait a bit and you'll soon enough know all, revealed to you over the best victuals and drink as the folk down here can prepare without the blessing of God's sunlight and the green things that sprout beneath it. They do the best they can, though, as you'll find out for yourself soon enough."

"'They?'" I echoed. "And who are 'they' who are providing all this?"

"Tsk, Hocker, hold your questions for a moment. Though I know a great deal, there's others who are fitter to provide you with answers, including the man who first told me all of what I know about this place. So come along now, as they're going about the raising of that submarine that sunk beneath you, and that should prove of interest to us both."

I stifled my feelings of resentment and followed him out of the chamber. Like all the other mysteries that had preceded it, the current one would apparently have a gradual unfolding as well. If nothing else, all my adventures thus far were providing me with an excellent schooling in the art of patience.

Down a long corridor we passed, the damp walls of which, like the room in which I had awakened, were lit by crude torches that emitted a cloying, resinous smoke along with their sputtering light. I noted that the torches were mounted in brass fittings that, as with the ornamentation of the machinery aboard the, submarine, were based upon ancient British and Celtic motifs. The elaborate, intertwined designs, despite all the craft that had gone into their making, now seemed oddly funereal, like the devices upon the tombs of a dead race. The sight of them produced in me a feeling of oppression such as I had felt only once before in my life and that was when Ambrose by his powers had transported me to that chilling spectacle of a ruined London, over-run and murdered by the Morlocks at the very end of Time itself, I shuddered, feeling the cold air of the passageway go through my bones and into my soul, then hurried along behind Clagger.

After many turnings, the corridor at last opened onto a great cavernous space. It was the shore of the underground ocean opposite that from which Tafe, Clagger and I had, set out in the small boat. Its dark, scum-laced waters looked no less foreboding from this side. If anything, it seemed more so, due to my present knowledge of how close I had come to death while crossing it. The still water seeped through the cracks and crumbling ridges of the, ancient masonry that formed its boundary.

"Hocker!" I turned at the sound of someone calling my name and saw Tafe striding across the shore toward me. She now had once again all the appearance of confidence and strength that she had possessed above ground. It was as if by having faced her most inwardly dreaded doom – death by suffocation in the thick and vile waters of the underground ocean – the fear itself was conquered. The sight of her, albeit still in male disguise, was the brightest torch my faltering spirit could have perceived in these, light-starved depths. How much better, it struck me, to have a woman as your comrade rather than as the fawning admirer and house-slave that so many men of my generation unfortunately insist upon! Surely in the future, if there was to be one, such an improvement in attitude would be universal throughout society.

At Tafe's side was a strange figure of a man. Obviously he had once been quite tall, but advancing age had bent his reed-like frame so that the weight of his upper torso was almost entirely supported by the staff clutched in one gnarled hand. Wisps of silvery hair trailed back to his shoulders, and his skin, through being long away from the sunlight, had paled to the translucency of the finest waxed parchment. Tafe curbed the length of her stride so that the old man could keep apace with her as they approached us.

Clagger stepped forward and clasped the old man's free hand in both of his own. "So you thought you had seen the last of me, eh?"

"Hm, well, in this life perhaps." The voice was surprisingly rich and firm, a young man's baritone rather than the fluting geriatric quaver I had expected. "Though I suppose it's a common failing of old crustaceans like us to think upon the end of things too soon." The affection and respect that flowed between the two men was easy to discern.

"Hocker," said Clagger, turning and pulling the other figure toward me. "May I present to you Professor Gough Felknap of Edinburgh University?"

"Late of Edinburgh, I'm afraid," amended the old man. "Late of most people's memories, too, I suppose – however many there are that reach so far back." His red-veined but still clear eyes regarded me.

"Felknap..." I mused aloud. "Of Edinburgh? I seem to recall... must have been before I was born, though I think, I read of it. Wasn't there a stir about your disappearance? And your hall porter accused of your murder, or something like that?"

"Ah, yes, poor Weskind. I didn't mean to get the poor fellow in trouble. Managed to get a letter to an old classmate of mine on the Bench and that got the case dropped, but of course by then an unfortunate air of mystery had been created about the whole thing. Most regrettable, really." He shook his head at the memory, then glanced back at me. "And so you're the leader of this little expedition into deep territory, eh?"

"I could hardly say that," I protested. "I seem to have gone through more of a muddle than anyone else to reach this point."

"Nonetheless, young man, you bear a heavy responsibility." Felknap's keen eyes studied me closely. "Destiny – with perhaps a little assist from Dr. Ambrose – has called upon you for a great service to your land and queen. It is still Victoria up there, isn't it?"

"You know that as well as we do," said Clagger chidingly. "Eh... Just making sure. Things tend to get a little... hmmm... *confused* down here." He laughed and jabbed the edge of his bony elbow into my ribs. "As you've no doubt noticed."

"Frankly," I said mildly, "I don't have the vaguest notion of where I am or what's going on here. I take it you are acquainted with Dr. Ambrose. You do intend to enlighten me as he would, don't you?"

"All in good time, all in good time," said Felknap. "A lot for you to absorb, young man, and if there's anything I remember from lecturing at Edinburgh it's not to expound faster than ears can take it in. Courage, my lad; all things will be explained presently. But do step down this way a bit. I believe they've just about got their grapples down to the submarine, and I want to make certain it comes up all right. Come along, then."

The three of us, reunited once more, followed Felknap along the crumbling brickwork. "How are you feeling?" asked Tafe.

"Quite well, thanks," I said. "I suppose I owe a bullet-less brain-pan to you."

"Forget it. And don't relax just yet. We're not exactly in a safe harbour down here, you know."

"What do you mean?"

She looked away, her face set in a grim expression. "Just be careful, all right?"

"There, see?" Ahead of us, Felknap halted and pointed a thin arm out to a distant point on the water. "They're bringing it up right now."

I looked and saw a cluster of small boats, perhaps the same ones that had hunted down the hapless Morlocks. As I watched, the men in the boats continued hauling up the numerous ropes that plunged down into the dark water. At last the curved oval of the submarine's top surfaced in the midst of the boats. Rivulets of water ran off the metal plates as several of the men threw additional grappling hooks at the submarine's projections.

"Good, good," murmured Felknap. "Fine work these fellows do."

Without warning, the submarine's immersed bulk shifted, and several of the ropes holding it snapped. The vast bulk below the surface tilted, pulling the ropes out of the grasps of the men. More hooks, thrown in desperation, failed to halt the abandoned submarine's slow descent, The last ropes parted and the curved shape disappeared beneath the water.

"Pity," said Felknap. His age-contorted body sagged with disappointment. "They did all they could, I suppose. It's hard to keep ropes in good condition down here, what with damp and rot getting into them. But it is a shame, though, to lose that submarine. It was the finest of all the Atlantean artifacts in the Grand Tosh." He sighed, looking regretfully at the spot where it had vanished. The boats were wheeling about and rowing back toward the shore where we stood.

"Excuse me," I said. "But did I understand you correctly? Did you say 'Atlantean?'"

"Oh. Yes. Quite." He nodded for emphasis. "The craft was quite ancient, I assure you."

"But– Atlantean? I had no idea…"

"I imagine not, young man. Like most educated people, I considered the story of Atlantis to be a mish-mosh of unfounded legends and confused references to other parts of the world. But that was before I made my way down here and discovered the evidence to the contrary."

"The submarine?" I said.

"Oh, much more than that," said Felknap. "Indeed, my dear fellow, you're standing in part of Atlantis right now, or at least a far-flung outpost of it."

"But I thought– I thought it was called the Lost Coin World, or something like that."

"Aye," said Clagger beside me. "That's what I told you, and that's the name the toshers have for it. Because, you see, they've heard of the place and think it to be where all the coins and valuable things that are never found even by them eventually drift down to. Only a few of the oldest and wisest toshers working the sewers of London know what's really down here."

"And that is?" I asked.

"Well, now," said Felknap, "you might not credit it in such a gloomy environment, but I have a chamber nearby where we can talk in comfort. I've several casks of salvaged malmsey as well to aid in the exposition of pertinent matters. Excalibur as well is tucked away in a safe place there. Shall we?" He pointed to one of the torch-lit tunnel openings that flanked the shore.

"Lead on," said Clagger quite cheerily.

As our little group followed behind the professor, I looked back to where the small boats that had attempted to reclaim the submarine were now rowing up and being tied to iron posts set in the man-made shoreline. Even from this distance I could see the sharp looks of suspicion and distrust on the pale faces of the men. I hurried after the others as a deep foreboding stirred in my vitals.

"Permit me to ramble on unchecked for a while," said Felknap as he poured a thick stream of wine into the goblets before him. "An old man's prerogative, and a professor's as well." He looked up and noticed the attention with which I was studying, the goblet he had pushed toward me. "Ah, yes, solid gold that is. A lovely piece of Atlantean craft, you know."

"The designs," I said, tapping a nail upon the side of the goblet. "Those intertwined, serpentine knots. Quite a resemblance to the ancient Celtic arts."

"Indeed." He nodded approvingly. "Many of the old Celtic traditions have their origin in the lost culture of Atlantis. Not that the Celts are descendants by blood of the Atlanteans, of course, but there was a considerable amount of trade between the two peoples once. The Celts, being far less advanced than the Atlanteans, were able to absorb the superficial art motifs, but naturally none of the technology that could produce something such as that submarine. If I had a chalkboard I could make a proper lecture out of all this, I assure you. But to continue.

"I first became interested in the legends and rumours concerning certain remnants of the lost Atlantean culture that were supposedly somewhere beneath London while I was still at Edinburgh University. After much investigation I tracked down the source of these stories to an old drunken sewerhunter who had been driven away by his fellow toshers for using the cover of the sewers' darkness to practice certain loathsome vices–"

"By God," interrupted Clagger, "toshers are as high minded a bunch as any of the rest of mankind."

"Yes," said Felknap, "more's the pity. At any rate, this banished fellow had wandered north to try his luck in combing the sewers of another city, but had chanced to come upon an equally lucrative and more pleasant occupation. In return for food, beer – mainly beer – and a doss in one of the hall's cellars, he regaled the Edinburgh undergraduates with his preposterous ravings about the so-called 'Lost Coin World', and all the treasures that had drifted over the ages down into its keeping. The students regarded him as an entertaining loony and nothing more, and the entertainment value was wearing a bit shabby when I at last located him. I had to fuel his thirst in order for him to consider my questions, but his answers, when wrung dry and studied, were of the utmost intrigue to my mind. With a shaky pen he drew some of the designs and ornaments he had observed during his sojourn in the Lost Coin World, and their specific similarity to ancient Celtic motifs was easily beyond the poor sot's power of fabricating by himself.

"Was he an agent in some elaborate hoax? Or had he indeed seen such things far below the city of London? Be it a fragment of Atlantis or not, such a find would be of considerable archaeological importance. Secure in my professorship at the university, I was nevertheless bitten by the viperlike lust for fame. So I travelled to London on my sabbatical, leaving my initial informant behind as in his liquor-fogged state he would have made a poor guide, and sought my passage through the London sewers."

"Twas me very own father he engaged to lead the way," Clagger informed the rest of us.

"And a fine man he was, too. Here's to his memory." Felknap took a long pull at his goblet and his listeners followed suit. The malmsey's warmth spread across my chest, fighting away the chill of the underground. "Yes," continued the old professor, "Moses Clagger led me straight and true to this very region, and told me all he knew of it as we travelled. He introduced me to his friends among the inhabitants of these depths, and arranged with them for my comforts and assistance in my research. At first I intended to stay but a few days or at most weeks, but when old Moses recrossed that great water he left me on this side." He drained his goblet and sat back, gazing into its glowing interior.

"You mean," I said, amazed, "that you've been down here all these years, without once returning to the surface?"

The silvered head nodded. "When first I came the gloom and damp and the weight of the earth above all quite oppressed my spirit.

But I was soon caught up in my research and was as comfortable as if I were turning pages of some tome in the cosiest niche of the British Museum. For you see, I had found my life's work down here. These Stygian depths are the field upon which the seeds of my genius have been sown. The burning passion of the scholar, though it has nearly consumed my life, has nonetheless kept me warm down here. Though all this is but the tiniest fragment of the glory that Atlantis must once have been before its destruction, still this fragment is a richer, more rewarding object for my attention than all the much-handled bones and potsherds that were ever scrabbled up from the surface's dry dust. Think of it – Atlantis. And *I* found it." An immodest pride thickened his voice.

"There's no doubt of it being Atlantis?" I said.

"None whatsoever, my dear Hocker. I've managed to do some rough translations from a few of the runic inscriptions that were left behind by the departed Atlanteans. Their import is quite clear. This complex of underground chambers and tunnels once formed a sort of way-station in a network of subterranean passageways that once extended beneath most of the European continent. And perhaps even farther than that; an obscure reference exists to the most distant terminal in the network being located in the roots of the Tibetan mountains. All of these tunnels were constructed by the ancient Atlanteans with their lower depths filled with water, the temperature of which was ingeniously regulated so as to provide separate currents running in either direction. Submarines, such as the one with which you, Hocker, became so regrettably, acquainted were the devices used for transportation.

"A quite remarkable race were these Atlanteans. Their achievements and ambitions far outstrip ours. Indeed, only the greatest of geological calamities was able to vanquish them. Those who were not on their native island when it sank below the Atlantic apparently soon passed away in grief for their drowned brethren."

"All the Atlanteans died?" I gestured at the stone walls around us. "Then who are these other men who live here in these depths? I had presumed them to be the descendants of the lost race."

"Unfortunately, such is not the case." Felknap paused to refill his goblet and to pass the cobwebbed bottle among his audience. "The present inhabitants of these regions are the descendants of a band of London sewer-hunters who migrated to these depths back in the Eighteenth Century. Finding things more congenial here among the decayed trappings of a dead race's past glory than up amid the squalor and general hard times of London's top side, they elected to stay. Can't say I would blame them for their decision – there's no sense in viewing that shabby period of English social history through a veil of nostalgia.

"There are a couple of species of strong-flavoured fish that are unique to this locale, plus an abundance of what is euphemistically termed 'straight-tailed pig' – that's rat to you. Some of the wet slimy things that grow on the walls can be scraped off and prepared quite tastily. All in all, these people have conducted themselves with typical British ingenuity. Rather like a band of Robinson Crusoes lost on an island under the Earth. Some of the original pioneers made a brief topside expedition in order to fetch their wives down here. This little unknown outpost of Queen Victoria's empire has had all the civilised amenities."

"Quite a thriving little colony, then," I noted.

Felknap shook his head, the long silver strands of Ibis hair catching at his shoulders. "I'm afraid not. The rigours of an underground, sunless life didn't agree with most of the women and with very few of the children born here. On the whole, the group is dying out. I very much doubt whether there will be any of them still living after another ten or fifteen years. No, the successful – if you wish to call it that – adaptation of Man to a subterranean existence lies in the far future with the rise of the Morlocks that are now besieging us."

"You've had contact with them down here?" My heart stepped up a pace at the thought of our enemy and their clandestine activities.

"Oh, yes. It was quite unavoidable that some of the men should meet up with them. The Morlocks are making their preparations on quite a large scale. In the regions of the sewers that they've taken over are enormous stockpiles of weapons and supplies to be used in their invasion of the surface world. They apparently intend to erupt all over London and the surrounding areas simultaneously. And at the centre of their hoard of armaments is, of course, their doorway ahead to their own time – that cursed Time Machine which is the root of all this evil."

"You've seen the Time Machine?"

"No," said Felknap. "But I've had reports of it from some of the men down here who have become familiar with the Morlocks. What they've told me about it, in addition to what Dr. Ambrose has related to me, is the extent of my knowledge concerning the device."

His words aroused an uneasy feeling in me. "Do you mean to say that some of the people down here have dealings with the Morlocks? Fraternise with them?"

The age-gnarled hands gripped his goblet tightly. "I'm sorry to say that that has indeed become the case. Over half of the men have gone over to the Morlocks completely, serving the invaders as guides through the sewers and the like."

"For God's sake – how could they? Can't they see the extent of the fatal enmity that exists between our race and the Morlocks? How could such traitors come to be?"

"Tis a shameful revelation," muttered Clagger. "A stain upon the honour of them that hunt the sewers, that their deepest kin should do such a thing."

Felknap nodded, his seamed face cast in a mournful expression. "True," he said. "But the darkness and the cold down here can slide all around a man's heart and freeze it as tight as an Arctic rock. When you live in these deep regions it becomes harder and harder to remember your brethren who still live under the light of the sun. Those men who cast their lot with the Morlocks at last thought that they saw more of a similarity between themselves and the Morlocks than with the human beings of the surface. The others, who haven't given their allegiance to the enemy – I don't know. They've always been a taciturn lot, not much on voicing their thoughts, so I can't tell whether some scrap of loyalty to the human race still resides in their hearts, or whether they simply dislike surface men and Morlocks equally. Ah, whichever it is, it's a sorry condition for men to have let their hearts sink into."

My hopes of finding allies among these subterranean residents seemed effectively dashed by the old professor's information. Tafe and I were still essentially alone on our mission, with a sick, perhaps even dying Arthur waiting for us above, Ambrose beyond any chance of assisting us, and Clagger and Felknap capable of little more than guidance due to their advanced ages. A hopeful thought formed in my mind. "Couldn't it be," I asked Felknap, "that you are misjudging the ambivalence of these remaining men? Perhaps the Morlocks inspire in them an intenser loathing than you suspect. After all, didn't they surround and kill the Morlocks who abandoned the submarine when it sank? Surely that says something about their attitude toward the invaders."

"Yes, but not what you think. As far as that incident is concerned, the men were simply taking revenge on the Morlocks for their having stolen the submarine in the first place. The men are quite passionate about what they call the Grand Tosh, which is the great store of valuables that were left here by the Atlanteans or have drifted down here from other parts. A bad business, that of the

Morlocks sneaking into here and making off with the submarine, not to mention kidnapping someone to pilot it. Now that a good number of Morlocks are dead because of it, the blood-lust of the men is pretty well satisfied. The only fortunate aspect of the affair was that the men were out on the water waiting for the submarine to surface, and thus able to rescue Tafe and Clagger when your boat was capsized."

I was by now sufficiently convinced of Felknap's statement of the underground dwellers' sentiments. "There's nothing for us to do here, then," said I, "but to fetch the copy of the sword Excalibur that is in these people's possession and return with it to the surface."

The old professor's hands knotted and clenched once more. "I fear it's not as easy as all that."

"You mean they won't give it to us willingly?" Despite my bristling words, my heart was sinking. Fatigue and the underground gloom were sapping my strength. I felt little in the mood for violence or subterfuge in order to get the sword. "We have the authority of the one Excalibur we already possess.

Wouldn't these men see the rightness of re-uniting the swords and returning them to the hand of the king whose weapon it is? Surely the name of Arthur, Lord of Britain, bears a little weight with them."

"Perhaps it does," said Felknap. "They are not so far removed from their British heritage as to have forgotten it. And perhaps they would willingly give you the sword – if they had it."

His last words struck me like a blow to the throat. "Doesn't it reside in this Grand Tosh you spoke of?" The flaring light of the torches on the wall dimmed at the edges of my vision. Was this entire dismal trek to turn out fruitless at last? Worse than fruitless – every delay meant so much more time for the Morlocks to ready their invasion plans unhindered.

A look of shock had burst forth on Clagger's face. "You told me the sword was here," he said in a piteous strangled voice. "When I sent me nephew to inquire of it, he returned with your message that the sword was down here in the Grand Tosh."

"And so it was – then," said Felknap grimly. "That was before the defection of the

greater part of the men over to the side of the
Morlocks. Acting on the orders of their new
masters, the traitorous men removed the
sword from the Grand Tosh and handed it
over to the Morlocks. From what little communication I've had with those who did it, I
now fear that the sword is now no longer
anywhere here in the sewers at all!"

"The Morlocks have taken it to their own
time?"

"That is my well-founded suspicion. But as
to what the Morlocks' purpose may be in re-
moving it hence, I have no idea."

I mulled over this latest, most bitter revelation. What was the import of such a
manoeuvre on the part of the Morlocks?
Could it be that they no longer considered
the bowels of the Earth below London to be
a safe enough hiding-place for this one copy
of Excalibur? But the only thing that could
have prompted such a fear in so arrogant a
breed would be if they suspected our efforts
to retrieve all the Excaliburs and field them
back into the one true sword. Had Merdenne then eluded the trap by which
Ambrose meant to remove him from the
scene and thus prevent our plot from being

discovered? The questions whirled about in my mind at a faster and faster rate, driving all my hopes and fears before them like chaff on the wind.

"Looks bad," said Tafe in her usual laconic manner. Her face betrayed no sign of tension, yet I knew that her thoughts were on the problem as frantically as mine were.

"Even if we were lucky enough to gather together all the other Excaliburs," I mused aloud, "it would do no good without this one that's lost to us now. And bloody well lost it is, too. The Morlocks have the only Time Machine, and thus the only access to that sword, and we have no hope of winning past the Morlocks without Excalibur restored to its true power and in the hands of Arthur again." I fell silent, the rigid obstinacy of the conundrum before us paralysing my means of speech. The darkness was spreading through my heart, the darkness that would soon swell, fester and cover the Earth if no spark of light could be found in this blackest of times.

All my recent efforts and exertions were catching up with me now, as though all

along the poisons of fatigue and weariness
had been draining into this low point and I
had at last stumbled into the bottomless pool
they formed. Perhaps an Arthur, a true hero,
could battle on and on without rest or respite
but a mere human such as I would feel the
effects sooner or later. My very bones felt
tired, limp from the pervasive damp and
chill. It's one thing to face great odds, but
even the smallest struggle, if undertaken
without hope, looms and swells with the
fatal poisons of despair.

I could tell that Tafe felt the same way,
though she had intimated nothing like this
aloud. She sat in a corner of the chamber,
empty now except for the two of us, gazing
at the drained goblet in her hands without
seeing it.

Idly, I reached and drew the cloth-
wrapped bundle across the table toward me.
Felknap had brought our poor Excalibur
from out of safekeeping and left it with us
while he put the exhausted Clagger to bed.
What the old professor's motives were in
doing so was unclear to me. I lifted the bundle in my hands, the wrapping stiff and
darkened from immersion in the dirty waters

of the sewers. The cords that bound it slipped off easily and the cloths fell away, leaving the blade exposed to the chamber's flickering torchlight.

What an unholy conjunction of science and magic had weakened the ancient weapon! Even in its diminished state, its rightful power leeched away by its cruelly distant duplicates, it was still an impressive vision. The gleaming metal of the blade shone red as blood in the torchlight, and the jewelled eyes of the twin serpents that coiled about the hilt sparked with the same fire. Enough could be made of the obscured runic engraving on the blade to catch-the mind as one's fingers ran along the fiat of the weapon. An evil work was that which had clouded over these sacred letters. When would they be read again, and understood by the eyes for which they were meant? The hand that by ancient right should be holding this weapon might even now be clutching at the failing heart that staggered in an old man's chest.

I was aware of Tafe watching me as I gripped the sword's haft and held it out before me, the cutting edge uppermost. So much seemed to balance on that fine line slicing without moving through the thick noisome air. Not the least of the things poised on the blade's edge was myself. Which was it to be? I could set the blade down and creep away ashamed, to die here or back on the surface, no matter which. Or on the sword's other side lay more pain and effort and perhaps even a crueller death at the end of it all, with not even the faintest glimmer of hope that the trials would accomplish anything at all. Nothing to sustain us in the battle but our will and a faith so blind as not even to see how dark the valley was through which it passed.

Though treacherous cunning had made the sword only a quarter of its true weight, its burden was still heavy in my outstretched hand, and my arm began to ache from holding it out before me. I gazed down its gleaming length for what must have been an even longer time, then lowered it carefully down onto the wrappings spread out on the table. As I retied the cloths about the sword, I looked over at Tafe's waiting face.

"An idea has occurred to me," I said almost casually, though my heart was beating wildly in my chest at the closeness of the decision between life and living death. "A plan, perhaps," I went on. "Tell me what you think of it…"

9

Morlock Hospitality

"Go straight down this tunnel," said Professor Felknap, his gnarled hand trembling as it pointed the way. "It'll be quite a distance, and a good deal fallen down toward the last part. Just pick your way over the rubble until you come to a T, then go right. If the rats give you any trouble – they're bigger in these parts – just wave your torch at them and they'll back off. You'll see the lights of the Morlocks' encampment, if they don't come upon you first."

I nodded as I lifted Excalibur, now wrapped in fresh cloths and bound with leather straps onto my back. The familiar weight of the sword felt encouraging across my shoulder blades. "Very well," I said. "Turn right at the T. I doubt that we'll have any trouble finding them."

"It might be better for you if you did get lost on the way." The professor's lean face lengthened as though weighted down by his forebodings. "This plan of yours strikes me as being little more than a short walk to your deaths."

"Have you some other plan to propose?"

"No," he said. "You know I don't. Maybe if I thought about it more…"

"There's no time for that," I said. "Who knows how many days or hours we have left? Either Tafe and I take our chances with this scheme, or we can all creep back into the lowest hole of the Lost Coin World and wait for death to come."

"Go, then." Felknap clasped my hand for a moment. "It's better to risk it on your feet then stay back here with two such tired old men as Clagger and myself."

"When he's recovered his strength," I said, "send him back up to the surface to look after Arthur. I have no idea how much time our little adventure will take before we can return to the king."

"Yes, of course I'll send Clagger. And I'll have watch kept for you here – when you come back this way."

"Let's go," said Tafe impatiently. She lifted her torch to the opening of the tunnel.

"Good luck," called Felknap after us. We were only a little ways into the tunnel and I could see its circular opening behind us, and no longer the old professor's worried face.

A pair of small red eyes appeared near my feet, then disappeared with an angry chittering noise and a scrabble of claws as I waved my torch at them. Tafe walked on before me, leading the way to our rendezvous with the Morlocks.

In my mind I reviewed the scanty details of our plan. It held no carefully mapped-out course of action for us. Little more than an opening gambit it seemed, which would thrust us into a game with fatal consequences for the smallest error.

The reasoning behind my plan was this – Dr. Ambrose had not reappeared upon the scene, as he surely would have if he were able to. There was every indication that he knew his way around these depths below London. So his continued absence could mean either that his plot to keep Merdenne bottled up was still in effect, or a grim thought – Merdenne had somehow managed to overpower

Ambrose, dispose of him for good, and return to an unhindered career of master minding the Morlocks' invasion. If the latter were true, then there would indeed be no hope of achieving our goal, for what chance would we have against Merdenne, forewarned and beyond any interference by Ambrose?

But if both of these powerful figures were still absent, then there was a small thread of hope which we could perhaps follow to success. For with Merdenne suddenly gone, surely a state of some small confusion had arisen among the Morlocks. Not enough to prevent their invasion of England and the world beyond – that would still undoubtedly go off after only a small delay. However, the retrieving of the Excalibur duplicate from its original hiding place in the Grand Tosh indicated – at least I hoped it did – that a degree of uncertainty had crept into the Morlocks' knowledge of the situation.

Our enemy had no way of knowing that a plot was underway to reunite the scattered Excaliburs, as Merdenne would not have revealed his setback at our hands to his confederates. Now that the schemer was not about to contradict us, it was my intention to present Tafe and myself to our enemies the Morlocks, and claim for ourselves the distinction of being Merdenne's lieu-tenants. A lie as audacious as that held some chance of succeeding, if only by the sheer magnitude of it. We also had one of the Excaliburs to back up our claim. How, I intended to ask of the Morlocks, could we have gotten possession of such an object unless we were indeed important associates of Merdenne?

A simple reversal of facts would suffice to explain the sudden departure of Merdenne from the scene: to prevent *Ambrose* from in-terfering, Merdenne had worked a spell to keep them both trapped in a distant time. In his absence, Tafe and I were acting as con-ductors of his orders to the Morlocks.

From there onward our course would have to be played by ear, so to speak. It would be useless to anticipate the twists and turns our lies would have to take in order to succeed in winning the confidence of the Morlocks. If we managed to do so, we would then invent some pretext for reuniting our Excalibur with the one in their possession, and then somehow attempt to get away from

them with it. Two more duplicates of the
sword were hidden somewhere else in the
world! I put these out of my mind, so as not
to have my heart quail at the enormity of the
task that lay before us.

Our easy progress down the tunnel soon
came to an end. Small fragments of rubble
grated beneath our bootsoles and we held
ourselves carefully as the footing became
even more precarious. Soon the rubble
mounted into great banks filling the tunnel
from side to side. Over these we crawled,
holding our torches before us as well we
could. One pile of shards was so high as to
leave only a foot or so of space between it and
the roof of the tunnel. We slithered through
the gap on our stomachs. Something in the
darkness behind us nipped at my ankle as I
went through, but I shook it loose and was
gratefully on the other side.

A pool of stagnant muck had collected
against the opposite wall of this dam, and it
was through this we waded knee deep hoping no pitfall was concealed beneath the
slimy surface. So inured had I become to
the foul conditions of the universe that
these sewers and passageways formed, that

I was scarcely aware of the ordinarily nauseating odour that was emitted by the decaying matter in the water. A portion of my mind, though, ticked steadily away, longing for a hot bath and a cologne-scented Turkish towel. With one hand I touched the swaddled Excalibur on my back, and pressed on.

The passageway came to an end. On either side similar tunnels branched off. This was the T section to which Felknap had directed us. Tafe gestured with her torch to the passageway to the right, and I followed behind her.

Evidence of some kind of directed activity was apparent as we went. The floor of the tunnel had been drained, with small gutters dug along the sides to carry off any water that did collect. What rubble there was had been carefully swept from the centre of the passageway.

Tafe stopped suddenly and held up her hand. "I hear something," she whispered, turning her ear to the tunnel's far end.

After a few seconds of silence, the sounds were noticeable to me as well. Mechanical noises as of engines, combined with scraping and sliding. Supplies being moved about, perhaps? Voices as well, shouting out orders and directions, though I could hear those only faintly. In the sewers' odd acoustics it was impossible to tell how close we were to the Morlocks' subterranean beachhead.

We resumed our progress. On one hand, we wished to proceed as cautiously as possible in order to see as much of the situation as we could before entering into it. However, we also wished to present as confident an aspect as possible to any of our enemy that chanced upon us. A show of timidity would seal our fate as securely as an outright admission of our true identities and plans.

The noises grew steadily louder as we neared them. I could make out the harsh gutturals of the Morlocks quite distinctly, the sound of their bestial voices raising a tremor of loathing along the skin of my arms. I fought the feeling down, reminding myself that I had to present myself as a friend to these creatures.

The tunnel turned to one side. From around the corner we could see a dim bluish light seeping. This illumination, I surmised, was probably that which the Morlocks found least painful to their sensitive eyes. We were almost upon them in their covert stronghold. I braced my backbone and positioned myself at Tafe's side as we walked toward the light of our enemies.

No sooner had we turned the corner than a chorus of basso shouts sounded all about us. Figures leapt out of their hiding places in the passageway behind us and brandished their weapons at our backs. A similar horde of Morlocks, outfitted in the same type of drab military uniforms as the others of their breed I had seen, arranged themselves in a semi-circle before us. Even if we had wished to, there was no possibility of escape from them.

The ugly band, their squat-fingered hands shading their eyes from our torches, jabbered at each other and growled at Tafe and myself. The sight of so many of their loathsome, death-pale faces swimming around me aroused the keenest nausea in the base of my stomach. The feeling was not relieved when the largest of the Morlocks, with a wrinkled face, presumably from age, resembling the bottom of an unbaked loaf, pressed the point of his bayoneted rifle against my abdomen.

I drew myself as erect as possible and glared at my captors. "See here!" I blustered, injecting as much fire and steel into my voice as I could. "What the bloody hell is the meaning of this! Get that rude pig-sticker out of my gut this instant or I'll have you cleaning out every sordid privy between here and the abyss. Do you hear me!"

The Morlock's eyes grew even more saucer-like as he goggled at me. Under the onslaught of my barking he drew back the point of his bayonet and stood in mute befuddlement. His startled companions had fallen silent as well.

"The same goes for you, horse's ass," said Tafe to the one who had brought his bayonet up against her stomach. "Put it away or get ready to eat it." Her threat seemed clear to him despite his lack of English. With a much deflated expression on his pasty face, he took away his weapon and turned to the leader of his little troop for further orders or simple reassurance.

Standing in front of me, the wrinkle-faced one looked me over dubiously. Clearly we were not any of the men from the Lost Coin World. Who then, he was obviously wondering, could we be? And our behaviour was equally puzzling to him. Not only were we not visibly afraid, we were doing our best to seem imperious and disdainful of the whole ugly lot of them.

The mental effort proved to be too much for the leader of the Morlock patrol. I almost felt sorry for the creature as, with a frankly bewildered expression, he dispatched one of the group toward the light and noise farther along the tunnel's length.

"Very good, my repulsive friend." I nodded approvingly at the Morlock. "I trust the superior for which you sent has a greater command of English than you do."

"Ghrah?" He made the little beseeching noise deep in his wattled throat.

"That's right. You keep telling yourself that and everything will turn out fine."

"Look at this little toad over here," said Tafe. "Isn't he a beauty?"

"Lovely." The face of the one in question swung toward me as I spoke. "Reminds me of a Pekingese my maiden aunt once had."

Several minutes passed as we discussed the varied features of the motley crew surrounding us. We made no move to get past them, as

Tafe and I agreed that such an attempt might cause panicky defensive measures on the Morlocks' parts. Better to wait and confront the personage for whom the wrinkled sergeant had sent.

As the time lengthened, though, doubts began gnawing my confidence from within. What if the band's superior refused to come and see, but simply issued an order to dispatch the unknown intruders? What if Merdenne had indeed escaped from Ambrose's trap and was here, already aware of our every intention? These and a host of vaguer fears moved through my thoughts. If the Morlocks managed to perceive them, our little confidence game would be over.

At last, footsteps and voices sounded from down the tunnel The Morlock who had been sent reappeared, jabbering excitedly as he trotted along at the side of a much taller, striding figure.

As this new entity approached us, I could see that Ambrose's information about there being different types of Morlocks was correct. This one, being taller, lacked the squat, toadlike body shape of the others. The same flaxen hair flowed down the neck, but the death-pale face had a higher forehead and thinner lips and nose. A marked degree of intelligence showed in the great round eyes as they flicked from my face to Tafe's and back again. Clearly this was a member of some intellectually superior variety of Morlock, fit for directing the activities of his brethren less gifted in mental capacity. As befitted his position of command, various insignia were displayed upon the shoulders and breast of a finely tailored uniform.

"About time you got here," I said sharply to the figure as the circle of Morlocks parted at his arrival. He stood in front of Tafe and me, his jack-booted legs spread wide as be looked us over.

I lowered my brows and returned his stare, curling my lips into a haughty expression of disdain. His eyes met mine and held for several seconds as his pale forehead furrowed in puzzlement over the enigma we presented to him.

At last he spoke. "Who are, you?" he snapped. "What are you doing here?" There was a heavy accent to his deep pitched voice, as though the inflections of our English were unsuited to his vocal mechanism.

"Come, come," I said in feigned exasperation. "Merdenne told me you people ran a slipshod operation down here, but this surpasses all my expectations. You mean to tell me you've made no preparations for our arrival?"

The Morlock's suspicious manner did not dissipate. "You had best explain yourself," he said in his slow, grating voice.

"Of all the—" I shook my head and sighed in disgust. "Merdenne told you nothing of our coming here?"

"What do you know about Merdenne?"

"Apparently more than you, my good man. I am in possession of his latest instructions concerning your little, ah, manoeuvres down here, shall we say? And if you value your rank you'll bloody well pay attention to what we've come here for. There's quite a genuine little crisis going on, if you're not aware of it yet, and it's going to take some unusual measures to ward off disaster for us all. Do you understand my words?"

The procession of thoughts behind the Morlock's eyes was almost painfully obvious. He at last decided to fish for more information. "Please explain," he said in a slightly more polite manner, "what it is to which you are referring."

"My dear fellow," I said, "I'm not about to stand here surrounded by your little hooligans with their rusty pikestaffs, and try to explain a very complicated situation to you. My colleague and I have already tramped through miles of loathsome wet sewers to reach your wretched little camp. I'm not acquainted with the amenities of your colony, but we would both like large containers of hot water, soap if you have it, though that seems doubtful from the aroma of your platoon here, and as decent a hot meal as you can provide. I'm not expecting every refinement but damn it all, man, this invasion is a civilised business, and we should conduct ourselves accordingly, don't you think." I lifted my chin and gazed down my nose at him.

The word *invasion* evoked a noticeable response from him. For a moment the large circular eyes goggled a fraction of an inch larger at me. It was now clear to him that we were privy to the purpose of the Morlock's presence here beneath London. Were we indeed allies of whom he had heretofore been ignorant? Or simply well-informed adversaries? The possibilities moiled around behind his eyes.

"Well, come on then," I said impatiently. "When Merdenne gets back he won't be very pleased to hear of these uncalled-for difficulties you've put us through." A scrap of doubt was still visible in the Morlock's face. "Very well. I don't much care for waving this about among a crowd of underlings, but if there's no other way of convincing you…"

I unstrapped the bundle from my back, brought it in front of me and undid the cloths. The mob of lesser Morlocks stood on tiptoe to see, pummelling each other into silence. Across my outstretched hands lay the sword Excalibur, an awesome sight even in its weakened condition. The blade reflected the available light, gleaming like dark glass over the deepest fires of the Earth.

The Morlocks, after several moments of gorging their saucerish eyes, stepped back a respectful distance from Tafe and myself – all except the tall, commanding one. He stood facing us, a new element having entered the calculations running through his head. "How did you come to have that?" he said, after a few seconds.

I began wrapping up the sword again. "Well, well," I said, "now just how do you suppose it came into my possession? Do you think I'd have it if I wasn't very well supposed to have it? Merdenne put it into my keeping, obviously." I tucked the bundle under my arm and glared at our interrogator.

"Why did he do that?"

"See here," I ground out, my face rigid with anger. "I'm damn well sick and tired of your infernal time-wasting inquisition. There's a bloody good reason for my having this thing, and it's going to be on your head if all our plans are fouled up. So just you trot along and lead us to the things I requested. There's a lot to be done."

The last shred of his scepticism wavered in the face of my onslaught, then was gone. He nodded respectfully, turned and snapped out orders in his guttural native tongue to all the other Morlocks. They scurried down the passage toward the dim blue light ahead of us.

"This way, sir," said the now obsequious Morlock. He pivoted on his heel and led the way. Tafe caught my eye and delivered a large wink over her triumphant grin. The

gambit's initial moves had succeeded – but
what of the rest that remained to be played?

The Morlocks, as it turned out, were already
anticipating the comforts they would derive
from the conquest of the England far above
their heads. The Morlock officers – for they
were entirely organised on a military basis –
enjoyed a great many comforts that Merdenne
had arranged to be sent down in devious
ways from the better London shops. The regular Morlock soldiers, of course, lived in the
same rude fashion as common fighting men
through all times and places do, and expect to.

In the apartment of Colonel Nalga, the
Morlock officer whose confidence we had
won, I luxuriated in a steaming hot tub,
soaking away the accumulated filth and
grime from our long sojourn in the London
sewers. A decanter of Fortnum and Mason's
best port lay near to hand. I lavished the cake
of Pears over myself, forgetting for a moment
our precarious situation as I wallowed in the
sheer animal pleasure of hot water and soap.
Adventures, I reflected, are all very fine but
a certain amount of civilised comfort forms
the true kernel of our desires.

At last I emerged from the bath, my heart considerably cheered and rededicated to the preservation of our English values.

A patented safety razor still in its box lay on the wash stand, and with it I tidied the edges of my beard. When my toilet was completed the face that peered back at me from the looking glass was undoubtedly my own, but changed somehow. The nearness of death, which even now was hovering close at hand, had burnt away the juvenility of my face, exposing the hard, decisive bones beneath. Or so I fancied – others simply might have thought that I hadn't been eating on a regular basis, and been right, too.

During my bath my clothes had been sponged, mended and pressed by the colonel's valet. Not a bad job of it, either. Very likely the Morlocks had had time enough to learn how to handle stains from the sewer's effluences. I dressed and sauntered out, sighing and drawing upon one of the fine Havana cigars the valet had placed in the breast pocket of my coat.

Tafe and Col. Nalga were waiting for me in the drawing room of his quarters. "Mr. Hocker," said the Morlock officer, smiling and fingering one of the insignia on the front of his uniform. "Your colleague Mr. Tafe and I were just discussing the – what is the word? – *details* of your journey down to our little encampment. I feel I must apologise for the inconvenience of our location."

"Think nothing of it," I said magnanimously, waving the fumourous end of my cigar in a grand gesture. "Hardships are only natural in time of war, what? Soon enough we'll be conducting our business from inside the House of Lords itself! A bright future awaits us, Colonel." I spotted the wrapped Excalibur lying on a sideboard. Picking it up, I saw that the distinctive knots with which I had bound it were still intact. I had been a little uneasy at first in trusting it to the Morlock, but had finally done so in order not to appear suspicious. Apparently my decision had turned out for the best.

"Let us hope so, Mr. Hocker," said Col. Nalga. "The preparations continue even as we stand here and talk. The unexplained disappearance of Merdenne has caused some confusion but we have maintained our efforts. We are even a few days ahead of the original time schedule that was set up for the invasion, and the assurances that you have given us that nothing is amiss with our trusted ally Merdenne will be a further boost to the morale of the lower ranks. As you say, things will soon be very different." His ghastly pale face split into a smile like that the Mongol invader must have worn when he first spied the unspoiled fields of Europe.

"Quite commendable indeed," I said heartily, although my spirit was chilled by his words. *Ahead of schedule* – how much time then was left? I immediately regretted the slothful half-hour that I had spent soaking in my enemy's bathtub while a whole green world ran down the drainpipe. "I'm sure," I continued, addressing the Morlock, "that the work of individuals such as yourself will not go lightly rewarded."

He returned my courteous half-bow. "Living space for my people is all the reward I desire to see. In the far future this globe is under our entire dominion. It is merely our destiny to rule it through all the past and present as well. I'm glad that there are a few individuals of your breed who have the foresight to recognise this."

"Indeed." The scope of the creature's ambition, presumably shared by all the members of his race, touched a cold base in my spine. Here was our enemy's face nakedly exposed. "My fears are, however," I said, "that all this elaborate preparation will be of little value if the current crisis facing us is not speedily resolved. Merdenne, the guiding hand of so much of our efforts, is already engaged in turning back the attempts of certain forces who wish to hinder our plans. Of one of them you may have heard – the one called Dr. Ambrose. If there were more time available to us I would explain the nature of Merdenne's present struggle to you. Suffice it to say that his presence is needed elsewhere. So sudden was the onslaught of our foes' machinations that there was, as you have noted, no time to inform his allies here of the need for his absence."

"It sounds like a grim situation," said Col. Nalga with rumbling graveness. "What can we do to assist him here?"

"Unfortunately, very little. The success or failure of Merdenne's fight against our enemies depends almost entirely upon his own powers. There are certain things he needs, though, and Mr. Tafe here and I have been dispatched by him on the errand of fetching those items out of hiding and bringing them back to him. Without them there is little chance of his winning the day against our foes; with them his victory and later ours is assured. Quite a simple matter really." I puffed on the cigar, adding tobacco smoke to the verbal haze I had created in the room.

"And, Mr. Hocker, what are these items?" said Col. Nalga.

"This is one of them, right here," I said and lifted Excalibur in its wrappings. "The three other copies of this sword that were produced through the agency of the Time Machine are now needed as well by Merdenne. That is the errand Mr. Tafe and I have come upon."

"I see," said Col. Nalga, sombrely. "Doubtless Merdenne needs the swords for some magical purpose?"

"Correct. At first he believed that it was sufficient merely to keep the swords out of the hands of Dr. Ambrose, but it has now become apparent that they must be actively employed in our behalf. I am aware that you have had your friends from the Lost Coin World turn over to you the sword that had come into their possession—"

"That was a decision from higher up in the chain of command," interrupted Col. Nalga. "It was felt by some of our generals that, given the unexplained absence of Merdenne, it would be wise to secure the sword someplace more under our control than the Grand Tosh. Hence its removal by our allies from there."

"A wise decision," I said, "given the circumstances. In matters such as this it's a good thing to be cautious. But that necessity is at an end now. If you will produce the sword we can start our journey back with it to Merdenne."

"Yes, of course." The Morlock officer nodded. "However, the sword is not right here at hand, but it is only a shaft distance away. We put it in the safest hiding place we could think of. I'll take you to it right now, if you'll care to follow me." He stepped to the door and opened it with a courteous bow. After following us out, he led the way from his quarters.

Our luck had held so far. The Morlock officer had communicated his belief in our statements to his higher-ups and our claim to being Merdenne's assistants had been accepted without a qualm by them. My spirits were greatly elevated at the prospect of successfully completing this stage of our quest with so little difficulty. Much still lay before Tafe and myself to be done, but at least the hope of accomplishing it had returned to my breast.

Col. Nalga led us out of the officers' complex – several Morlock lieutenants and other officers saluted as we went by – and past the enlisted men's barracks. The enormous space that the Morlocks had excavated belied the fact that it was so far under the surface of the Earth. Somewhere above our heads Londoners were going about their business, all unaware of the desperate gambles we were pursuing beneath their feet. How I longed to be with those solid citizens in the English sunshine, or even the good cleansing rain, once more!

Past the towering stockpiles of supplies and weapons went our little procession. Scores of the squat-bodied, less intelligent Morlocks were sweating like navvies as they scurried to and fro, pushing pallets of crates across the cavern's floor. Col. Nalga stopped and pointed with pride to the furious activity and the enormous amount of the stores.

"You see?" he boasted. "And this is only the smallest fraction of our preparations. What chance do the puny surface dwellers have against an invasion force such as this?"

I managed to suppress any sign of the chill that had condensed in my vitals at his words, and smiled back at him. "No chance at all," I agreed. "When Merdenne finishes with this small affair, I'm sure you'll sweep across England like a tidal wave." My own words felt nauseating in my throat.

We went on toward the very centre of the Morlock encampment. Beyond the barracks and the stockpiles was an open space with a large square building in the middle of it. "This is where you're keeping the sword?" I asked as we approached the construction. "Seems rather conspicuous for a hiding place, don't you think?"

An enigmatic smile formed on Col. Nalga's pallid face. "There is more to it," he said quietly, "than what you can see."

With a key attached by a long chain lanyard to his belt, the Morlock officer unlocked a large panel on the side of the building and drew it aside. In the dimly lit interior I could make out the form of some type of mechanical apparatus that was the only thing occupying the space. "What is this contraption?" I said, somewhat annoyed. "I don't see any sword here."

"Patience, Mr. Hocker," said Col. Nalga. He lit a lantern that hung down from the ceiling of the building. By its light I could clearly see the details of the apparatus and recognised it instantly.

This was the Time Machine. Before us squatted the root of all the evil that had descended upon us, the device that had made possible the entry of a plague such as the Morlocks upon our green and undefiled land. My mind flew back to that long distant, or so it seemed, evening when the Time Machine's inventor had sat in his parlour and regaled his guests with the story of the Machine's creation and his subsequent adventures with it. The fool! If he had only realised what he was unleashing upon the world through his meddling with the laws of the universe. But no, he died happily ignorant of the final results, and it was left to us to reap the bitter storm whose seeds he had unwittingly sown.

After my first emotional reaction upon seeing the Time Machine, I was able to note the many details that gibed with its inventor's description of it to his audience. The saddle, the gleaming control levers, the faintly shimmering section that seemed somehow unreal, the finely detailed workmanship all reinforced my conclusion. This could only be the Time Machine itself. How long would it be before a restrengthened King Arthur stood where I was and plunged the true Excalibur into the Machine's metal and crystal vitals?

I suddenly realised that I had been staring at the apparatus for some time without saying anything. Col. Nalga was watching me intently when I turned to face him. "So this is the device Merdenne has told us so much about!" I gestured at it with one hand. "The scientific marvel that makes all our plans possible. I'm really quite pleased, Colonel, that you took the time to show it to us. You've satisfied a deeply held curiosity on my part, I'll have you know. But time is pressing, unfortunately, and I feel we should return to our business and move along to wherever it is you've hidden the sword. Shall we proceed then?"

The same smile as before moved across Col. Nalga's face like a thin cloud across the moon. "I'm afraid I didn't make myself quite clear, Mr. Hocker. I said that our copy of Excalibur was not here, but could readily be fetched. To dispel the mystery, the sword has actually been taken to the far future through the use of the Time Machine here. My fellow Morlocks up ahead in our native time period have placed the sword in their safekeeping."

Without wishing to, I blinked and stared at the Morlock officer. So Professor Felknap's suspicions had proved correct. "This– this is absurd," I stammered. "What's the idea of this continuous shilly-shallying about? I suggest you hop aboard that damned thing and go fetch the sword back here this instant!" My feigned wrath was the only cover I could create for the apprehension I felt at this new development disrupting the flow of events that I had been anticipating.

"Please control your anger, Mr. Hocker." Col. Nalga held up a mollifying hand. "Our desire to safeguard the sword led to our decision to remove it from this time and take it to our own. Surely there is no fault in that?"

"Perhaps not," I said, allowing myself to appear somewhat calmer. "But the moment has come to bring it back to this time, and with the greatest possible dispatch. Please do so. We'll wait for you here."

Col. Nalga shook his head with every indication of regret. I'm afraid that our generals have ordered a different plan. It is their wish for you to proceed via the Time Machine to our native point in time and pick up the sword yourself from them." He raised his shoulders and spread his hands to indicate his helplessness in the face of his superiors' edict.

"This is outrageous," I said, sputtering with exasperation. "We're here on direct orders from Merdenne himself, and we don't have time for this kind of foolishness from your lot of comic-opera generals. Just you go ahead and fetch that sword and if you need any defence for your actions I'll ask Merdenne to look after your generals as soon as he is able." I halted my outburst and glared at him with as much ferocity as I could summon. In truth, an overpowering fear of the Time Machine had sprung up inside me. The thought of being propelled by it through however many centuries lay between this time and that of the Morlocks filled me with the greatest apprehension I had ever felt. Our deception of them was apparently still in effect so I suspected no treachery on their part. But still I had no wish to sever the one link to normality that had remained unbroken through all the strangeness of the adventures through which we had gone.

"I'm afraid that's not possible," said Col. Nalga, his voice flat and obstinate. "I have my orders and I must follow them."

"Nothing," I said, equally insistent, "can induce me to have anything to do with that Machine."

"I have something here that might serve to change your mind." Unhurriedly he reached into the breast of his uniform and pulled out a pistol of dull black metal. He pointed the even blacker snout of the gun toward us and took a step backwards in order to cover the two of us better.

Before he completed the motion, I saw Tafe from the corner of my eye drop to the floor. The bark of Col. Nalga's gun echoed in the building as he fired at the half spinning, half rolling figure that came at his legs. The shot missed, and the next one rang against the building's metal roof as she collided with him. They fell together, each one's hands straining for control of the gun between them.

I ran toward the wrestling figures, but even before I could reach them panels on all sides of the building slid open. Revealed in the doorways was an entire squadron of Morlocks training their rifles upon us. "Hold it right there," said the officer in command of them.

Col. Nalga got to his feet, blood streaming down the side of his face from the place where a handful of his silvery hair had been torn out by Tafe. "Get up," he ordered her from behind his trembling pistol. She did so with a sullen, defiant air.

Blood seeped between Col. Nalga's fingers as he held his free hand to the side of his head. "Well, Mr. Hocker," he said, relishing his triumph. "Your little masquerade fooled no one. Chief assistants of Merdenne, eh? While we've known all along that you're both pawns of Dr. Ambrose! And in fact, we've been anticipating your arrival down here for some time. No, Mr. Hocker, your playacting has been a dismal failure. We're too many moves ahead of you in this game." He snapped an order to one of the Morlock soldiers, who then came up and tore the wrapped Excalibur from my grasp.

"How– how did you know?" I asked the question with what I expected to be my last breath. The squadron of armed Morlocks had stepped into the building and formed a tight, rifle-bristling circle about us.

"You'll see soon enough." He gestured to-ward the Time Machine, glittering icily in the centre of the area. "When you arrive at your, ah, *destination*. Shall we?" He stepped toward it, letting the crowd of Morlocks push Tafe and myself along behind him.

10
The Dark Castle

The experience of crossing the future centuries to the Morlocks' native time was much different from that which the Time Machine's inventor had described to the guests in his parlour so long ago. Frequent use of the Machine had, as Ambrose had explained to us, created a channel between our time and that of the Morlocks. As the device could now only shuttle between those two points in the Earth's history, the speed of passage was greatly increased. The dizzying rotation of night and day, even if we had been on the Earth's surface, would not have been perceived by us. It was only a brief, nauseating sensation, as when a ship drops beneath your feet during a stormy Channel crossing, and we had arrived epochs away from our original time.

Furthermore, the channel effect the Time Machine now possessed had also increased the amount of mass shifted by the Machine. Instead of just transporting a single rider upon its saddle and the small personal effects he carried on him, the Machine now took with it everything within a range of several yards. This was how the Morlocks had been able to move the enormous amount of supplies and weapons that they were stockpiling beneath London. Accordingly, Col. Nalga at the Time Machine's controls, Tafe, myself and a dozen or so Morlock soldiers guarding us – all arrived in the far future simultaneously.

As soon as the disorienting jolt to my system had worn off, I looked about the area to which we had been transported. The same dim blue light prevailed as in the Morlock base underneath the London of my time. A marked difference existed beyond that, however. Now the area had the aspect of having been well-established and used for some time by the Morlocks. There was no building set up around the Time Machine, so that I could see the space beyond it was not a crudely hollowed out cavern such as we had left behind us, but was instead an arched vault constructed of gleaming metal panels. Like a limitless cathedral it seemed to extend in either direction. Along one side several carts full of supplies sat on a track of metal rails, waiting to be transported into the past from which we had just come.

A group of Morlocks in slightly different uniforms stepped forward and took charge of Tafe and myself. We each had our wrists bound together with bracelets connected by a short chain. Our ankles were left unshackled so that we could walk. We were pushed away from the Time Machine until we were out of range of its effect. I looked over my shoulder and saw it shimmer, then disappear with the group of Morlock soldiers who had guarded us.

Col. Nalga stepped in front of us. The blood from the wound Tafe had inflicted on him had dried into a crust on the side of his face. His pallid visage twisted into a sneer of contempt as he addressed us. "We shall all see each other again," he said. "I have business to take care of at the moment, and then there will be much travelling – in space, not time – before you reach your final destination. But I promise you I'll be there. Until then." He gave a mocking salute to us and turned on his heel.

"Go to hell," said Tafe after him. One of our new contingent of guards scowled and barked an incomprehensible command at her. "You too," she replied.

Before the interchange of words could go any further, a length of chain was fastened to our manacles and we, surrounded by our Morlock guards, were led away. The procession made its way down the arch-ceilinged corridor until we came to a smaller passage branching off from it. This in turn led to a small room, hastily converted from its storage function into a cell. The chain and manacles were removed from our wrists and then we were shoved inside the bleak chamber. The heavy door slammed shut behind us. It opened again long enough for one of the Morlock guards to throw a couple of threadbare blankets inside, then closed with a decisive clang. Tafe and I were alone.

She paced the few yards that defined the room's width, then sat down on one of the

blankets. "Doesn't look too good, does it?"
she said, her voice almost casual.

"You have a succinct way of assessing the
situation," said I. "But I agree with you. This
seems to be pretty much the end." After a
few moments of reflection, my degree of self
control no longer surprised me. In a way, it
was a relief for the whole thing to be over.
We had given it our best shot. There had been
no action for which I now felt I could blame
myself. Perhaps Ambrose had erred in not
having picked someone of a more naturally
heroic mode for his purposes. But I had done
what I could, and felt guiltless. An infinite
sadness and regret was in me for the bitter
prospects that still lay ahead of the innocent
world I had left so many centuries behind. I
had no doubt, though, that that fate would
be shared soon by Tafe and myself.

Tafe's voice broke in upon my dark medi-
tations. "What do you suppose is going to
happen now?" she said. Her voice sounded
singularly unemotional. Perhaps she had arrived at the same inner judgments as I had.

"I have no idea." I gestured at the cubicle's
bleak walls, illumined by a single blue sphere
overhead. "Perhaps they have put us here

and already forgotten us. This might very well be our tomb."

"Didn't that Nalga say something about doing some travelling, though? I wonder where to." She mused on the empty space in front of her.

"Who knows?" I said. "Their motivations can hardly be credited as human. For all I know they may intend to ship us to some victory banquet they are planning, and to serve us on silver platters with apples in our mouths."

Our conversation ceased on that cheerful note. For a span of some hours we sat in gloomy silence, keeping our thoughts to ourselves. Starvation at least was not to be our lot, for one of the Morlock guards opened the door and deposited a tray bearing a carafe of water and a pair of flat, circular loaves of bread. After a moment's hesitation, wondering as to the origin of the food, we ate and drank. So passed an unknown amount of time, terminated when I at last fell asleep on one of the thin blankets.

The sound of the door being pulled open roused me from a dreamless sleep. Tafe was already sitting up with her back to one of the chamber's walls, regarding our visitor. I righted myself and saw that it was Col. Nalga standing in the doorway with his retinue of Morlock guards standing just behind him.

His repugnant sneer of victory was still congealed across his death-white face. "It seems," he said, "as if I'm not yet relieved of the responsibility for you. As I've brought you this far, it is now my duty to transport you somewhat farther."

"And where might that be?" I said with stiff formality. However many triumphs he might be anticipating for his noxious breed, the Morlock officer remained an insufferable upstart.

"You'll see soon enough," he said, the sneer turning into a wide and nasty grin. "If you two would care to step out into the corridor, our journey may commence."

As we exited the tiny room one of the Morlock guards stepped forward with the manacles and chain we had borne previously. Col. Nalga waved him away. "I think we can dispense with those," he said, turning toward us. "I'm sure you both recognise the futility of attempting anything rash."

Indeed, the close presence of the Morlock guards precluded any chances of escape. And beyond that, where was there to escape to? We were irrevocably stranded centuries away from any succour. Our captors' mercy – a laughable notion – was our only fate.

"Very good," continued Col. Nalga. "Come along this way, then." He led us to the lofty main corridor. There, on the metal tracks on which the carts of supplies ran to be loaded near the Time Machine, was a small passenger vehicle. Through its windows could be seen several upholstered seats arranged against its walls. An engine, not steam but some other type that emitted a low hum, was connected to the front of the little cab.

"Get in, please," said Col. Nalga as one of the guards ran ahead and opened the cab's door. Tafe and I mounted up a set of folding steps and took our seats on either side of the compartment. The elegant appearance of the vehicle was much diminished upon close inspection. The leather of the seats was racked and split open, and the dark wood panelling was warped where it was not actually peeling away. Apparently this, like the Atlantean submarine back in the Lost Coin World, was an item that the Morlocks had salvaged from the remains of some earlier people. Perhaps it was an artifact of the last true men before they had died out and left the world to the Morlocks and the effete surface people of which I remembered the Time Machine's inventor talking. No wonder that the Morlocks, incapable of creating anything themselves, wished to plunder an earlier world's creations and resources.

Col. Nalga and two of the guards climbed into the cab and took the remaining seats. The engine ahead whined and started to move. In a few moments we were rocketing, down the vaulted corridor at quite a heady rate of speed.

"I hope you're not alarmed," said Col. Nalga. "But we have a great distance to go, and patience is not the long suit of those who are waiting for us."

"You refused before to divulge our destination," I said. "Will you tell us then who it is we're going to see?"

"Forgive me for toying with you so cruelly. I don't wish to play cat-and-mouse with your questions and my answers, but I have my orders. Suffice it to say that you will soon be face to face with one who is not a Morlock such as I, but who nevertheless leads our plans to invade your time."

"Merdenne?" I said. "Is that whom you're speaking of?"

"Merdenne!" scoffed the Morlock officer. "That fumbler! Whatever happened to him he no doubt walked right into. No, he's not the one. But that's enough – I can say no more. Relax and enjoy this little excursion. It will soon emerge from this monotonous corridor and become more pleasant." He evidently relished the irony his politeness made in the face of our situation.

His words proved true in a short time. The little cab in which we rode reached a terminal point on the subterranean rail line, and we dismounted. An elevator, subject to stalls during its upward progress, took us to the surface.

It was late evening when we stepped out into the open air, but how good even the muted scarlet rays of the sunset felt upon my skin! My lungs drank in the air uncontaminated by the underground's clamminess and filth. The grim hope sprung up in me that, whatever the fate the Morlocks had in store for us, we would be allowed to meet it out in the open rather than in some fetid chamber in the Earth's dark bowels. A spasm of horror at the thought of an underground death coursed through me, then passed away as I forced myself to observe the landscape around us.

The Time Machine's inventor had described it accurately. This far-advanced age had transformed England into a sylvan park, the beauty of which belied the hideous activities of the Morlocks below the surface. Trees and lush-grown, rolling hills, and not one stone upon another to show that the great city of London had once stood here. All that was past.

"Where are... the other people?" I said. "I can't remember what the fellow said they were called."

"The Eloi?" said Col. Nalga. He and the group of Morlock guards had put on dark blue spectacles to shield their eyes from even the sunset's dim light.

"Yes, that's right. That's the name."

"I'm afraid that the fellow who told you of them actually observed our culture at a slightly earlier period than this. At this time we do not allow our valuable food source to wander freely around in herds. We use pens."

For a moment I was stricken with revulsion at this bold-faced statement of cannibalism.

But then I reasoned that it would make as much sense to accuse a lion or other wild man-eater of the same crime. An animal such as that seemed as related to us as the Morlocks were – that is to say, not much. No, the process of evolution had made them into a separate species. No matter what our common origins might be, they were a breed apart. And as such, if I could have raised my hand to strike down the whole lot of them I would have done so with no more remorse than that felt by some rural vermin-hunter of my time toward his prey.

As the skies darkened we proceeded a short distance to the bank of the Thames, now a clear, sweet-smelling flow of water rather than the refuse-choked lane of commerce it had been in my day. At a small dock a boat was waiting for us. We boarded and headed out to the channel. As the craft cut through the water I looked away from the gloating faces of our captors and up into the night sky. Over the centuries the stars had slowly shifted their positions. None of the constellations I knew from my time were still recognisable in the heavens. Those too were past, lost in the ocean of Time. Beside me, Tafe leaned over the rail and spat into the water.

I fell asleep with my back against the rail, and woke only when we reached the shore of the European continent. Another transfer was made, this time to a train much like the ones I had known. At its head, however, was the same oddly humming type of engine. Tafe and I were placed in a compartment with two narrow bunks in it. "Relax and rest yourself, dear friends," said Col. Nalga as he closed the compartment's door. "You have yet a long journey ahead of you."

The door proved locked from the outside when I tried it. The windows as well had been sealed over with a heavy metal plate, except for a small ventilation space at the bottom.

"Paranoid bastards," said Tafe. "What's so important that they don't want us to see?"

"Like most evildoers," I noted, "they have a penchant for needless secrecy. Fleeing when no one's pursuing, as it were." I laid down on one of the bunks and closed my eyes. The train's motion as it picked up speed lulled my thoughts. In a few moments I was back in the sleep I had started while crossing the Channel.

Dr. Ambrose was speaking to me, but I couldn't see him. All I could make out around me was a vast pattern of alternating black and white squares like a chessboard. I stood on one of the squares and in the distance other figures loomed, dark and mysterious. *Fear will lose the game*, said Ambrose's voice. *Take courage… take the sword…*

"Take it easy, Hocker! Just hold still and lay back. Jeez, are you awake?"

My eyelids fluttered, opened and I looked up into Tafe's worried face. Her hands were on my shoulders, pressing me back into the bunk. "What– what's the matter?" I said hoarsely.

"Where *were* you?" she said. "You were thrashing around and yelling 'What sword? What sword?' Like to scare me to death. What was all that about?"

"I– I don't know." The chessboard landscape was fading from my mind. "I thought I heard… No. Nothing. He must be long past, too, by now."

Tafe stared at me for a moment, then went back to her own bunk. I lay awake, listening to the train's passage through the night.

• • • •

We had two meals brought to us, of the same flat bread and water, before the journey was done. A full day – or two? – had gone by outside our sealed compartment, for it was night again when Col. Nalga and the Morlock guards took us off the train. Before leaving the little compartment they had given us heavy coats and fur-trimmed hats such as they themselves were now wearing. The reason for such apparel was clear as soon as we stepped into the open.

A freezing blast of wind struck us, flinging sharp, stinging crystals of ice into our faces. We braced ourselves against the arctic gale while our Morlock escort grouped around us. "What is this place?" I shouted to Col. Nalga through the roaring wind. All I could see was snow and darkness.

"We've travelled a long ways, Mr. Hocker," Col. Nalga shouted back. "Farther than you probably think. This area is in what was known in your time as Germany, near the mountain mass that was then called the Zillertal. The climate is considerably changed due to the advance of the Schleigeiss glacier."

Germany! Even in the numbing onslaught of cold, a shock ran through me on hearing this revelation. For what purpose could the Morlocks have brought us here? This seemed to surpass all the mysteries that had been generated so far.

"For God's sake," I asked, "what could possibly be here?"

"In your time there was only a small village nearby. That's all gone now, of course. If you hadn't had the misfortune to arrive in this storm you would have been able to see that to which we have come. But there!" He extended his arm, made thick with his heavy coat. "You can just make it out where it stands."

My eyes followed the direction the Morlock officer indicated, but at first I could see nothing. Then an outline took form, looming through the obscuring storm. Dark against the surrounding darkness, it seemed like some massive medieval fortification standing alone on the bleak crag above us. In all my studies I had never read of such a thing being erected in this remote area. Who could have built it in the centuries since my time, and for what reason?

The Morlock guards were at last assembled about us, and Col. Nalga led the way toward the towering dark shape. As we struggled toward it, staggering in the face of the wind and the snow, I could make out the sputtering glow of torches at a point near the castle's base. A few yards closer and I could see that they flanked a high-arched entranceway. Another group of Morlocks was there, awaiting our arrival.

We gained the shelter of the arch and could stand upright again. The storm beyond the stone walls continued to rage, blotting out any sight of the train that had brought us to this desolate landscape.

Salutes were exchanged between Col. Nalga and the Morlock officer in charge of the group that had been waiting for us. After a brief exchange in their own language, Col. Nalga turned to Tafe and myself. "You're in luck," he said, grinning malevolently. His pallid face beneath the fur-trimmed hat was as cold and heartless as the snow beyond. "You won't have to spend any time waiting. The one who ordered you to be brought here is ready to see you now."

"This seems as good a time as any," I said, then defiantly: "Lead the way."

With our previous guards behind and the ones from the castle before us, Tafe and I were escorted into the dark structure. By the light of the smouldering torches set at intervals in the walls I noted the castle's apparent great age. The stones that formed the walls were much battered and covered with time-worn inscriptions, and the stones of the floor were worn in channels from centuries of feet treading upon them. In all, everything about the castle gave an atmosphere of great antiquity and the solemn mystery that often accompanies old relics.

The corridor led to a wide stairway, the stone steps of which were similarly eroded by wear. The Morlocks halted and the group in front of us parted to form a passage between them. Col. Nalga came and bowed with mocking courtesy to us. "This way," he said, sweeping a hand toward the steps. We followed, I at least motivated by a desire to face the one who had so cruelly dashed our hopes.

The rest of the Morlocks were left behind as Col. Nalga, Tafe and I mounted the steps. We felt our way cautiously as the light from the torches in the corridor below was soon lost to us, and none were mounted on the walls of the stairway. Upward in darkness we proceeded, steadying ourselves on the uneven steps with our hands against the cold, damp walls.

At last Col. Nalga halted and raised a barely discernible hand. "The one beyond this door," he whispered, "is a person of great power and quick wrath. Guard your tongue, then, as it may mean a good deal of difference as regards the ease of your deaths." He pushed open the door he had indicated and motioned for us to go through. When we had stepped past him he did not follow but pulled the door shut behind us.

Not torches but a pair of candles partly illumined the chamber in which we now found ourselves. The wax tapers stood on a table close to the wall farthest from us. A figure sat at the table. In the dim light I at first thought it was some kind of a joke created by the Morlocks – a parody of an Egyptian mummy with a silk dressing gown wrapped about it. The figure's head was completely swathed in white bandages as were the hands resting on the table like ill-shaped parcels on a butcher's rack.

We stood motionless for several moments as we studied this gauze-wrapped apparition. Then it spoke. "Come closer. Where I can see you."

A shiver crawled over my flesh at the sound of the words. The voice, though somewhat muffled by the bandages, was oddly familiar to me. A woman's voice – where had I heard it before? I puzzled over this new mystery as Tafe and I crossed the room.

"So." The bandaged head looked up and studied us when we stood beside the table. "It's my pleasure to entertain the two of you again. Though I certainly hope you repay my hospitality better than the last time we met."

I could contain my curiosity no longer. "Who are you?" I asked, peering at the lines of the face concealed beneath the wrappings. "Why are you disguised in such a fashion?"

"Disguise?" A bitter laugh emerged from the gauze. I wish it were so." The white mass turned slowly from side to side as if the neck were capable of only limited and painful motion. "No," the woman went on, "the bandages are to keep my charred skin from sloughing off my flesh like leaves. Come, come, my dear Mr. Hocker. Was my fate so unimportant to you that you can't even recall a certain conflagration for which you were responsible? Such callousness from one who no doubt styles himself virtuous!"

"The clinic," I said, slowly realizing the truth. "Where Merdenne was keeping Arthur prisoner."

"That's right," affirmed the muffled voice. "Quite the little heroes then, weren't you? Rescue your precious doddering king, but leave a woman behind to die in the flames!" The bandaged hands flexed as if trying to curl into angry fists. "Are you saddened to discover that I survived?" A drop of spittle soaked through the gauze over her mouth with her bitter words.

"The nurse," I said. "At the clinic…"

"Ah, yes, the *nurse*, as you say. That was Merdenne's little masquerade for me. All the time I had served as his right hand, he wished to humiliate me that way. He knew my ambitions. were as great as his, and might someday cut the ground from beneath his feet. The wretch! Leaving me to die and rot in a hospital charity ward as soon as I had answered all his questions about your rescue of Arthur. I vowed then, in the heart of my scabbed and twisted body that I would live and take his place somehow. And so I have. Merdenne is gone and I am now the Morlocks' collaborator. The sweet triumph for which Merdenne craved will be mine."

The intensity of the woman's greed and egotism repulsed me. So Evil always had an understudy such as this to take its place when needed! "Do you know where Merdenne is?" I asked.

"It doesn't matter," said the woman. "From the fact of his sudden disappearance it's easy to surmise that your friend Dr. Ambrose has somehow managed to remove him from the scene. And since you two have been pursuing your quest without Ambrose's help, it's equally obvious that your powerful ally is also no longer a force that needs to be considered. No, the contest is between you and myself – and I have won."

"You knew then what we were trying to do? What the purpose of our quest was?"

The bandaged head nodded slowly. "After your raid on the clinic you had Arthur the King. What else would you need other than the sword Excalibur restored to its true strength?"

"So that's why you had the sword that had drifted to the Lost Coin World brought to you."

"Of course. But not just that sword. All of them I had located and retrieved, except for

the one that was already in your possession."
The woman's gauze-wrapped hands left the
table and lifted up something that had been
propped next to her chair. It was the sword I
had carried, still bound in its cloths and
leather straps.

The woman clumsily laid the bundle on
the table. "All along," she said, "I believed
Merdenne to be a fool for merely dividing up
Excalibur's power and scattering the swords
to their hiding places. A weapon such as this!
A thing of power! A waste for it not to be
employed to further our own ends. So after
I had taken Merdenne's place in the confidences of the Morlocks the first thing I
ordered was that the swords be found and
brought to this particular place."

"Why this place?" said I. "Of what signifi-
cance is this castle?"

"I'm glad you show a curiosity about
these things, Hocker. I would think it a pity
for anyone to die ignorant of the truth. As
for this place, it is a site of great power – the
same power that the sword Excalibur is said
to possess. The castle itself used to stand at
a similar site of power in the Languedoc section of France and was called Montsegur,

and before that Montsalvat. It was rumoured to have once been the repository of
that stone known as the Holy Grail.
Whether that is true or not I cannot say. Be
that as it may, a mysterious order that
called themselves the Last Cathars moved
the castle of Montsegur to this spot stone by
stone sometime in the last part of the Twen-
tieth Century – this I know from the records
they left behind. Their occult attempts must
not have been successful, for the order died
out and vanished shortly after. When I
learned of the existence of this place I resolved to bring the Excalibur swords here for
my own purpose – melding the swords into
one again."

Her last statement puzzled me. "Couldn't
that have been done anywhere? I thought it
was sufficient merely to bring the swords together and they would combine by
themselves into one."

A nod from the bandaged head. "So I
had thought as well. But I had three of the
four swords in my possession and nothing
resulted from their juxtaposition. They remained three separate swords, worthless in
themselves. That is why I brought them to

this desolate spot, hoping that the power inherent in the location and the very stones of the castle would serve to unite them."

"And you succeeded?"

"No." The word was hard and flat as iron. "Even in this place where more than anywhere else it should have been possible, nothing happened. I tried every conceivable positioning of the swords to each other, yet still they remained separate. At last I came to the only possible conclusion." She paused, then went on, her voice even more steely. "The swords are fraudulent. There is no Excalibur, and perhaps never was. It was all concocted by Dr. Ambrose for reasons of his own, most likely as a diversion to draw Merdenne's attention away from his real plotting."

Her accusation stunned me. "But– but that can't be– He told us. He sent us after them."

"So?" A shrug. "He used you then, a pawn on his board while his more valuable pieces awaited their turn. Did you really expect a master strategist such as Ambrose to move so simply toward his goal?"

For a moment I felt dizzy with shock, and Tafe put her hand on my shoulder to steady me. "I thought," I said weakly, "that he had told the truth to us. That he owed at least that much to us."

"You meant nothing to him," said the woman. "Such as you are less than dirt to him. But now I've grown tired of our little conversation. As I had expected, it was a rare treat to see your faces when I told you these things. Now you're so pitiful when deprived of your illusions that you make me sick." She raised her hand and the door behind us opened, admitting Col. Nalga and several of the guards. "Take them away," she ordered, then picked up the sword I had carried all through the regions below the Earth's surface, and tossed it into my hands. "Here – take your worthless scrap of metal. I hope you find it a fitting object of contemplation."

The Morlock guards led us out of the room just as peal after peal of muffled laughter sounded from the bandaged figure's hidden mouth.

Flight after flight of time-worn steps led down to the bowels of the castle. At last our guards had brought us to a heavy iron door with a small opening hatched over with bars. The flickering light of a torch was visible through the aperture.

"Consider this your last residence," said Col. Nalga, drawing open the door. The Morlock guards shoved us in, then the officer slammed the door shut once more. "I'm afraid," he said to us through the barred opening, "that whatever vermin you find in there will have to do for your supper. We hate to abandon our guests like this, but we must return to the invasion force that's massing beneath the England of 1892. Our plans will be ripe in a few days of that long ago time. So now we must leave you. Sleep well."

He and the guards departed, boots tramping upon the ancient stairs. That noise died in the distance above us. Tafe and I turned away from the door. There was no point in even trying it, as we had heard the bolt fall into place on the other side. We surveyed the chamber where we had been left to die.

From all appearances the room had once served as one of the dungeon cells for the castle. Below the sputtering torch on the wall dangled several pairs of rusting manacles and leg shackles. Most of the space, though, was taken up by the mounds of

nondescript trash that had accumulated in
this low point over the centuries. Old clothing and fetid garbage lay mixed in with
battered pieces of armour. Idly, I poked about
in the nearest heap with the cloth-wrapped
tip of the useless sword they had allowed me
to keep.

A trio of objects slid from the top of the
heap and clattered on the stone floor. In the
dim light I at first could not make them out,
but then saw that they were three swords,
all alike and identical to the one inside the
bundle in my hands. The Morlocks, having
found the sword useless, had simply thrown
them away down here. No doubt it fitted
their cruel mockery to shut us in with them
as well.

I disconsolately studied the swords as they
lay with their blades crossed upon each
other. So this was the end of our quest! That
which we had sought was now in our possession at last – a bitter treasure of lies and
useless forgeries.

Tafe came to my side and looked down
at the swords. "Kind of a disappointment,"
she said, moving one with the toe of her
boot.

"You might say that." The flat understatement amused some morbid humorist in my soul. "I'm not quite sure I would have come this far if I'd known it was going to be like this."

"Me either." For a moment I thought she hadn't caught my sarcasm, then I turned and saw her smiling sadly at me. "We gave it our best shot, though, didn't we?"

"Pity it has to end this way." I watched her foot move the swords about something about the torchlight glinting on the metal dropped into my mind like a stone into clear water. "Unless– "

"Unless what?" She looked at me, puzzled.

I turned and grabbed her by the arm. "See here, Tafe," I said excitedly. "That blood-thirsty woman upstairs couldn't get these swords she had to combine into one, eh? And so we all assume that Ambrose lied about them, and that they're incapable of merging back into one sword. But couldn't it be that these swords here, as they are only fraudulent copies of the true Excalibur that has always been in our possession, seek not to combine with each other but only with the master from whose mould they were taken?" I lifted the bundle up before us.

"Think of the true Excalibur as a glass filled with essence. These other swords need to be poured, so to speak, back into this one. Eh? What do you think of that?"

Tafe rubbed her chin thoughtfully. "Well," she said. "I suppose it's worth a try. We've got nothing to lose at any rate."

Hastily, I fumbled off the straps and cloths wrapped about the sword. When it was free of them I gripped its hilt with both hands, inhaled deeply, and pressed the point of its blade against the sword nearest to me on the ground. For a moment, metal touched metal with no result, then–

The torch on the wall flickered and nearly went out as a gust of wind pulsed through the chamber. In my hands Excalibur, now twice as heavy as before, suddenly pulled downward to rest its point on the dirty stone floor. Only two of the false swords remained beneath our eyes.

Tafe and I exchanged glances. "Go on," she whispered, her voice filled with awe at what we had seen. "Touch the others with it."

As I moved the true Excalibur toward the next sword I saw that the inscription on the blade had grown clearer, though it was still

blurred beyond reading. Metal touched
metal and another violent gust of wind
chilled our faces and hands. The sword
whose hilt I gripped was again heavier, having reabsorbed some of the power that had
been stolen from it.

One sword remained on the stone floor.
Slowly I brought the now weighty Excalibur
against it. The torch on the wall guttered
and went out in the sudden gust of wind
that filled the chamber. We were left in
darkness with the object which we had undertaken our quest to find: the one true
Excalibur restored to its full power. It lay
heavy in my hand as I lifted it and ran trembling fingers along the length of the blade.
The runic letters of the inscription were now
clearly incised.

I reached down to my feet and found the
wrappings in which I had carried it. I felt
now the sacredness of the object and the respect the ancient artefact deserved. When it
was bundled once more I turned toward Tafe
in the darkness and whispered, "We have
found it."

"Yes," came her reply. "But what good
does it do? We're thousands of miles and

God knows how many centuries away from the one who can use the sword. Arthur's back in the England of your time and we're in the middle of this Godforsaken frozen waste. Even if we could get out of this dungeon, how do you propose to get back?"

My joy at the restoration of Excalibur to its true state disappeared with Tafe's reminder of our condition. Our victory had again receded into shallow defeat. "Well," I said, my voice coming from some hollow centre of pain in my chest, "then there's nothing but– Wait! Did you hear something then?"

In the darkness it was easy to concentrate upon our sense of hearing. For a moment I thought it was perhaps nothing but the blood rushing in my veins, then Tafe spoke. "There," she said. "Something rumbling in the ground below us."

The sound grew louder, evolving into a churning, roaring noise. Soon the floor beneath our feet began to vibrate, and the ancient stones of the castle grated against one another. Dust from the long undisturbed roof sifted down upon us from above.

"What is it?" cried Tafe. "What's going on? An earthquake?"

The words of a half-forgotten dream came back to me, and suddenly I understood them. "No," I said, "it's the sword! It seeks to return to its proper time – and didn't the woman say that this was a place of power? Excalibur is turning the centuries back to the time where it rightfully belongs!"

With fearsome rumbling and groaning noises the walls of the castle began to crumble into their component atoms. The stones of the dungeon toppled in on us, but dissolved into nothingness before they hit us. Through the sudden yawning spaces above us I could see the moon and stars whirl about as they wrenched themselves back into the constellations of the year 1892.

"Hold on to the sword!" I cried to Tafe, thrusting the bundle between us. "It will take us with it. The power is great enough!"

Her hands grasped the cloth-wrapped sword. The floor heaved and creaked beneath our feet but we managed to stay upright. The stones of the castle lay all around in ruins, then flicked one by one out of existence as Time coursed backward.

the Earth's motion grew less, then finally was stilled. An eerie calm settled over the

snow-covered crag on which we found ourselves. Moonlight bathed the drifts, silvered
the trees of a forest below. Some small
mechanism of my heart felt at rest. This I
knew was the year 1892. Only distance separated us from England, Arthur, and the end
of our quest.

"There's still a chance," I said to Tafe.
"We may have arrived at a time early
enough to forestall the Morlocks' invasion
plans – if we can get Excalibur into the hands
of Arthur."

"Yes, but how?" she said. "That's hundreds
of miles away!"

"Col. Nalga said there was a village near
this spot. If we can get to it we can hire some
means of transportation to a larger town,
and then travel by rail back to England."

"Is there enough time for that?"

"What other choice do we have? Either we
go that route and pray we have enough time,
or we simply give up where we stand."

"No," she said, shaking her head. "We've
come too far for that. We'd better hurry if
we're going to find that village before we
freeze to death out here."

We commenced walking and were lucky

enough to stumble upon a well-marked trail leading down out of the hills. After following its winding length for only a half-mile or so we were able to spy a cluster of lights below us. We quickened our paces, longing for the sight of plain human faces.

Tafe suddenly spoke. "Don't turn your head yet," she whispered. "But when I say to, look about twenty yards up the face of the cliff just to your right, and be quick about it. All right, now."

I did as she directed and was rewarded with the sight of something being jerked back behind a little outcropping of rock. A death-pale face with white hair and dark blue spectacles! Perhaps.

"You saw it?" said Tafe.

"Yes," I said, nodding. "They're waiting for us here. When we disappeared from the castle in the future they must have reasoned that we had found a way to unite the swords and return with it to this time. Obviously they mean to stop us before we can reach Arthur with Excalibur."

"Let em try," said Tafe with fierce determination. "I haven't gone this far just to be stopped an inch from the finish line."

We made our way without incident to the little village at the foot of the hills. There I convinced one of the local burghers that Tafe and I were English tourists who had gotten separated from our hiking party. For a nominal amount of pound notes – my wallet had stayed in my inside coat pocket through all our trials so far – I hired a small cart and a pair of horses to draw it I promised to have them sent back by someone at our destination, which was the nearest town situated on a railway line. Another wad of notes secured the possession of two ancient, rust-specked rifles and a handful of rounds. "For the trolls?" said the seller, laughing as he handed the guns to me.

"Trolls?" I said. "What trolls?"

"Ach, some of the little children here claim to have seen trolls in the hills nearby. Pale white ones with blue glass spectacles. Such imagination they have!"

"Indeed," I murmured, and hurried outside to where Tafe was waiting with the cart.

"I'll take the reins," I said and handed her the rifles. "Load these and be quick about it. We'll need them before very long, I'm afraid."

The sun had not yet risen when we left the village. To reach our planned destination we would have to pass directly beneath a row of weathered cliffs that terminated one section of the hills from which we had descended earlier. This was the point at which I anticipated the Morlocks attempt upon us. I coaxed as much speed from the two venerable plow-horses drawing us as was possible, while the cart jarred in and out of the rural lane's ruts, shaking as if it were ready to fall apart.

For a moment, as we passed the last of the small cliffs that bordered the road, I dared to hope that the attack I had expected was somehow not to be realised. My small spark of hope was dashed when a pair of rifle shots sounded above us. The two startled horses bucked and reared at the noise, tearing the reins loose from my hands. One of the cart's wheels caught in a rut and twisted, snapping the worm-eaten axle. The cart crashed onto its side, throwing us clear and interposing itself as a temporary barrier between ourselves and any more shots from the cliff.

The bundle containing the sword Excalibur lay within reach of my hands. I drew it to my side, then gestured to Tafe a few feet away. "Give me one of the rifles," I said urgently. "They'll rush us soon – perhaps we can pick off enough of them to give us a chance to break for it."

"No," she said, holding the rifles close to herself. "Take the sword and one of the horses. I can hold them back while you head for the town."

"Give me the rifle. We're going on together or not at all."

"I can't go with you," she said, her voice straining. "Can't you see? I'm hit." She moved her arm away from her side and in the dim moonlight I could see the blood pulsing through her torn clothing and onto the ground. The two shots from the Morlocks had found their mark.

My mind swam dizzily for a moment at the sight, then held with decision. "I'll carry you," I said. "On the back of one of the horses. We'll be able to get away from them, and we can find a doctor in the town ahead."

She shook her head. "That's useless. I've bought it. I've seen enough of my buddies get shot in my own time, and I can tell how bad this is. I'd be dead from loss of blood in a mile and the Morlocks would catch up with you and kill you and take the sword and what good would it all be. Come on, get out of here. Take the goddamn sword and go."

I hesitated, then bowed to her wishes. "I'll send someone back for you," I said.

"Don't bother. I'll be dead by then." She winced from a sudden pain deep in her vitals. "That'll just cause trouble for you, and you've got to make time back to England."

Bending low to stay behind the cover of the overturned cart, I loosed the faster looking of the two horses from his harness. Under one arm I carried the bundle with Excalibur inside. "Good-bye, Tafe," I called back to her. "I– "

"Hey, are you going or not?" she said in exasperation.

I swung myself onto the horse's back, clutched my free hand into its mane, then dug my heels into its ribs. A hasty shot from one of the Morlocks kicked up dust at its hooves, but I was soon out of their range. I looked over my shoulder and saw Tafe lining up a shot over the side of the cart, then she was lost in the darkness behind me. As

I rode I leaned into the horse's mane, trying to press everything but my flight, from
my breast.

11
Mr. Hocker Sees it Through

I travelled by train all the way from Berlin to the Franco-German border in a state of high anxiety, unable to sleep or rest for fear of further Morlock attempts on my life. As well, the question of whether, after all my efforts so far, I would be in time to do any good preyed on my mind. Perhaps the Morlocks would have already launched their invasion from below London by the time I arrived... perhaps Tafe's sacrifice had been in vain and I was already hopelessly late, unable to forestall the horror... Thus my thoughts churned ceaselessly behind my brow, working through my brain like a fever.

An old school friend serving in the British Consulate was able, with a little cash to the right hands, to smooth over my lack of a passport. I explained Excalibur to the authorities as the result of an expedition financed by the British Museum to a distant Asian archaeological site. While the customs officials were debating whether I was a jewel smuggler, due to the ornamentation on the sword's hilt. I simply did smuggle it past with the assistance of an elderly Anglican clergyman returning from sabbatical. The old cleric carried it across the border under his cassock for me. Other desperately improvised subterfuges got me across France without arousing any more suspicions, and at last I was crossing the Channel to home. My dear England, unaware of the enemy laying their plans beneath the streets of its capital… The Dover cliffs were tinted red as blood with the waning light reflected from low clouds when we came into view of the coast.

My friendly Anglican got the sword past British customs for me – I had convinced him it was a sacred relic needing protection, which was not far from the truth. When we were safely past the officials I took the bundle from him and ran to catch the train for London without even a word of thanks for the old gentleman's help.

The last stage of my return journey was an agony of fretting and fuming at the train's slowness. Every second seemed like a drop of some precious fluid – life itself – that was spilling out onto the ground to be lost forever. When the train at last pulled into the station I pushed roughly past a pair of old ladies and knocked over a pram complete with squalling infant in my haste to dismount.

Outside the station I hailed the first hansom, gave the driver the address of Thomas Clagger's residence, pushed a sovereign into his hand with an injunction to hurry, and climbed in, bearing my precious parcel under my arm. I leaned back into the cab's upholstered seat, but was unable to catch my breath. Listening to the rapid clip of the cab-horse's hooves on the paving stones, I half dreaded to see an army of Morlocks come boiling up out of every sewer grate.

I took my gaze from the cab's window and saw for the first time that there was another person in the cab sitting opposite me. This was too much – the cabbie was apparently trying to increase his profit by carrying two fares at once. I could brook no delay caused by such an arrangement.

"See here, fellow," I exploded angrily to the other passenger. "I've given the driver express orders to take me directly to my destination. You'll have to get out and find another hansom."

"I think not, Mr. Hocker," said the other with a grim trace of amusement. At that moment we passed a street lamp and its flaring gas flame cast its light upon Col. Nalga's pallid face. A small pistol glinted in his hand, poised straight at my heart.

"You've given us quite a chase," said my enemy, relishing the expression of shock that crossed over my face. "I caught up with you in Berlin but couldn't get a chance at you by yourself. The first wave of our invasion is scheduled to be launched in barely a couple of hours, so naturally we didn't want any messy little incidents that could possibly arouse suspicion about our plans. Given the element of surprise, plus our superior numbers, there really isn't much of a chance for your kind – not without Arthur and the sword Excalibur to rescue them. So I'll just relieve you of that burden right now, if you

please." He extended his free hand toward
me. "Hand over the sword."

My mind raced feverishly as I slowly
brought the bundle between us. The hansom
driver, I realised now, was obviously a con-
federate of Col. Nalga, and would take no
notice of gunshot from inside the hansom.
The Morlock officer would have the sword
from me whether I was alive or dead. And
how much longer would I be allowed to
breathe after I gave it to him? A few minutes
for him to savour my defeat, and that was all.

Col. Nalga's hand reached for the bundle,
then drew back. "Unwrap it, please," he said.
"After the way you managed to restore it
and then cross all the centuries back to this
time with it, I really should put no limit to
your cleverness."

I undid the leather straps and pulled the
cloths from the sword. The naked blade lay
across my hands. Col. Nalga leaned forward
to verify it being the true Excalibur. As soon
as his eyes shifted from me to the sword,
my hand tightened on the hilt and I lunged
forward with it into his gut.

The report from his pistol echoed deafeningly inside the little space, but the shot

went wild and over my shoulder. As the Morlock's blood pulsed out along the metal, his pale fingers loosened their grip upon the gun. His breath rattled in his throat but I covered his mouth with my hand before it could break into a cry for help. The large eyes gazed at me for a few seconds, then filmed over. The corpse slumped sideways on the hansom's seat.

There were no street lamps in the section through which we were passing, so in darkness I pulled the blade free of its victim, wiped it clean on the dead Morlock's coat, then quickly re-wrapped it.

Watching from the side window of the hansom, I waited until the driver slowed for a corner, then slipped open the door and leapt for it, clutching Excalibur to my chest. I hit the paving stones with my shoulder, rolling until I fetched up against the curbstone. Bruised and shaken, I raised myself with a bloodied hand and watched the hansom careen out of sight, the driver apparently unaware of my exit. When he arrived at his destination with only Co. Nalga's corpse inside, the other Morlocks would soon guess what happened.

Not a moment to spare. I got to my feet with Excalibur clasped tight in my hands and ran, more by instinct than reason, through the dark London alleys.

My breath came in ragged gasps and a bloody salt foam was on my lips as I pounded on the door of old Clagger. I pounded again after only a few seconds, stopping only when I heard hurrying footsteps on the other side of the door.

Astonishment spread across Clagger's wrinkled face when he pulled open the door and saw me, an apparition of wild-eyed anxiety and shivering fatigue. "Mr. Hocker" he cried. "You've come at last."

"Yes," I said, shoving my way past him into his well-lit parlour. "And I've got the sword." I raised the now dirty and blood-stained bundle before his eyes. "Where's Arthur? Take me to him at once!"

Clagger drew away from me and his face mottled with Fear. "He– he's much worse," he said slowly. "I'm afraid– "

"Never mind that." I raised the bundle and brandished it. "This is the power to restore him – the true Excalibur!" The old man gestured toward a door and I turned away, opened it and stepped through with the hard-won prize.

The room on the other side was lit by a single candle at the side of a bed. "Arthur?" I said, stepping forward in the faint circle of light. "I have it. I've brought the sword to you–" Suddenly I fell silent as I perceived the occupant of the bed, his shoulders and head raised slightly on a bank of pillows. A grey, necrotic pallor had crept across the old king's sunken cheeks. Shallow, pain-filled breathing lifted the thin chest below the blankets. Two filmy eyes moved slowly upward to my own face.

"Arthur," I said mournfully. The truth was obvious. I had come too late. The old king was dying, beyond the help of Excalibur or any other power.

"Your king is checked," said Merdenne, lifting his hand from the piece he had just moved. "And mate? Yes, I believe so."

"Are you sure of that?" said Ambrose. He made no move toward the chessboard. "Are you sure there's nothing about which you may have been deceived?"

Something in the other's confident tone caused Merdenne's brow to crease in puzzlement. His eyes returned to the board, studying it…

"Hocker," said the figure in the bed in an achingly frail voice. "Come closer."

I stepped up to his shoulder, and stood gazing into his ravished visage.

"You have the sword? The sword Excalibur?"

"Yes," I said, lifting the bundle and showing it to him: "I'm sorry– "

"No, no," His voice cracked with impatience. "Unwrap it – quickly."

I did as he asked. The blade glinted in the candlelight as it lay across my palms.

"Read the inscription," he commanded.

Sick at heart, I turned the blade to my eyes. For a moment I didn't see it, as my mind was filled with a vision of the Morlocks, Unchecked, ravaging the green English countryside. All was lost, down to the last little spark of hope that had remained alight in my heart.

"Read it," came the quavering voice again.

I shook off the doleful vision and focused upon the blade in my hands. The ancient runic letters danced in the dim light, then froze as my eye caught hold of them. They seemed to leap from the blade, and the world swam dizzily about me.

Take the sword…

Some time later – years, centuries, compressed into seconds – I looked from the blade into the old man's eyes. "Yes," he said solemnly. "Now you know the truth. It is in fact only General Morsmere you see dying here. You are Arthur. Excalibur is your sword to use."

I knew he spoke the truth. The runic inscription on the blade of Excalibur was the key that unlocked my true identity. For one lifetime I had been Edwin Hocker; for many lifetimes before I had been Arthur. King of Britain, Saviour of Christendom. My sword lay in my hand. The deed to which I had been called from the world beyond this one lay far below my feet.

"Why did you and Ambrose deceive me, old man?" I said, my voice now great and terrible.

General Morsmere's withered face looked up at me without fear. "The sword was stolen by Merdenne and diminished in its power before you ever had a chance to see it. Yet you were the only one who could be called upon to find all the swords and merge them back together into one. Ambrose enlisted me in his plot to masquerade as King Arthur, and thus throw Merdenne off your trail. As I was already dying of consumption, Merdenne was easily persuaded that his reduplication of the sword by using the Time Machine had a weakening effect on Arthur himself. But as you see, you have succeeded in your quest; Excalibur is a key to power, not the power itself."

"But couldn't Ambrose have simply told me I was Arthur? Why deceive me as well?"

"Would you have believed him?" said the old man, smiling faintly. "No, for Edwin Hocker was a rationalist and a sceptic. It took a great deal to convince him that there was a King Arthur reborn, let alone, that he himself was England's resurrected hero."

"Yes," I said, gripping the sword tight in my hand. "But now I know."

"Yes," breathed the old man. The effort of explanation had exhausted him. Only a little time was left before his death. "Go now and vanquish the invader, as in the past you have done. You are one, and they are many. But most will flee before your coming, as your power is great. Go." He collapsed back against the pillows.

I left that place, leaving behind one old man dying and another bewildered, and retraced my way to the sewers' entrance. There I descended, sword in hand, into the most secret bowels of the Earth.

And then there was much shedding of blood in the darkness below the surface. Only those who know not killing would sing of such. It is an old tale, that of metal against flesh, to such a one as I. The armies of the Morlocks were advancing upwards when I met them. The old man's prophecy was correct – most fled at the sight of my grim visage and ran shrieking back into the safety they thought they would find in the depths. They knew that to cross Excalibur meant their deaths.

A few, braver or more desperate, stood their ground. I fought past them, heedless of the shots they managed to aim in those close quarters, and at last stepped over their fallen bodies as I continued downward to the root of the evil cancer at the Earth's heart.

And finally came a time when none, of the Morlocks stood before me. I stood in the chamber of the Time Machine, having made my way through all the remembered passageways and across the bridge the Morlocks had erected over the underground sea. The gleaming apparatus stood in the dim light, a mute witness to Man's ingenuity in creating havoc with the Universe. I raised Excalibur and struck deep with it into the shining metal and crystal.

The one blow was enough. Silently the cosmos flowed back together, knitting up the wound the infernal device had created. The dim light vanished and I knew that all the scattered Morlocks, dead and alive, were gone, returned to their rightful place in Time. All was as it should be now. The just order of the Universe was restored. My task was finished.

Suddenly a wave of weakness engulfed me, and I tottered and nearly fell. I pressed my hand to my side and found a warm wetness pulsing out of my many wounds.

On my will alone had I reached this place. My life's blood was even now ebbing from me. I sat down with my back to the chamber's wall. My arms and legs felt heavy and immobile.

Then Ambrose came to me in that place. The destruction of the Time Machine had liberated him from the trap where he had bound Merdenne. I knew it was him, the old friend and guide that in other times I had called Merlin, even though I could see nothing in the darkness.

"Well done, Arthur," he said, but why was he whispering?

My own voice sounded far away. "I don't feel very much like Arthur now," I said plaintively. "I feel more like Edwin Hocker again."

"He was a good man," said Ambrose. "A pity he has to die with you. Arthur will return, I and even Merdenne will return countless times, but Hocker's life is over."

"I don't feel bad about that," I said. Somehow the darkness about me was growing even darker. "But I do feel sorry for poor Tafe. I don't quite see why she had to die."

"You've forgotten. She came from a time that is yet in the future. She has yet to be born and has a whole life to live in a world free from the Morlocks."

"Yes. Of course. I'm not thinking too well now." Where were my hands? I couldn't feel Excalibur in them. "She… she'll be the same person, though, won't she?"

"She will," said Ambrose. "But in a brighter time."

"And a holy terror, I wager, to anyone who crosses her. I'm glad Hocker got to know her. He was really quite lonely a lot of the time." Something moved inside me that made me gasp, but the pain soon passed away. "I'm very tired now. Perhaps you'd better go."

"Yes. And I'll take the sword with me."

I could hardly hear him, or myself. "What will you do with it?"

"I will cast it into the underground sea here, so that it might return to you when you have need of it again. Farewell." Then he was gone away from me.

Only a little time had passed when the darkness folded about me like the softest and warmest of shrouds. And then, in that time and place – our Lord's year 1892 in Victoria's England – I saw no more.

About the Author

K. W. Jeter attended college at California State University, Fullerton where he became friends with James P. Blaylock and Tim Powers, and through them, Philip K. Dick.

Jeter wrote an early Cyberpunk novel, *Dr. Adder*, which was enthusiastically recommended by Philip K. Dick. Jeter was also the first to coin the term "Steampunk," in a letter to *Locus* magazine in April 1987, to describe the retro-technology, alternate-history works that he published along with his friends, James P. Blaylock and Tim Powers.

As well as his own original novels, K. W. Jeter has written a number of authorised *Blade Runner* sequels.

He currently lives in San Francisco with his wife, Geri.

www.kwjeter.com

K W JETER,
MORLOCK NIGHT

Adam Roberts

There is no single English word for "writing the sequels to a classic novel by a conveniently dead popular novelist"; but there ought to be. Plenty of writers have done it, and as an activity ("classicaposthumosequelizing") it has proved particularly popular in the world of SF. After all, more than most genres, science fiction is determined by its backlist of classic texts. New SF novels inevitably written in dialogue – openly or covertly – with the masterpieces of the genre's history. Writers insufficiently knowledgeable about the traditions of SF are condemned to a belatedly tedious process of re-inventing the wheel. Writers less ignorant know that their alien invasion story, or robot story, or generation starship story must deal with the many previous iterations of that theme.

Take, for example, time travel. A great Nile of SF novels, stories and films has flowed from one source: H G Wells's superb 1895 novella *The Time Machine*. It is (as of course you already know) the story of a man who propels himself out of time and into the future. In the year 826715 he discovers that human society has divided along divergent evolutionary roads: on the one hand, the useless, foppish nineteenth-century aristocracy have become the brainless, useless Eloi, existing in a purposeless idleness in the future's sunlit green spaces; on the other, however, the proletariat have degenerated into the subterranean, dark-adapted, monstrous Morlocks. Wells' story reveals that these latter literally prey upon the former, coming out at night and carrying them belowground to eat them. Whether this can be described as cannibalism is surely a moot point (since the Eloi and the Morlocks are separate species, it is perhaps technically not so); but it is a horrific narrative revelation for all that. Wells's story ends with the time traveller returning to his own time, but pausing only long enough to pass on his story before returning to the future with the intention of intervening to help the beautiful and helpless Eloi.

As befits so influential a text, various writers have produced various unofficial sequels to Wells's time travel adventure – both novels (Christopher Priest's *Space Machine*, Steve Baxter's *The Time Ships*) and films (one of Trek-director Nicholas Meyer's early cinematic offerings, 1979's *Time After Time*, brings Wells's Time Traveller and Jack the Ripper to 1980s Los Angeles). But none of them have the brainboggling, wigged-out splendour of K W Jeter's 1979 proto-Steampunk masterpiece *Morlock Night*. There's a reason for this, I think, and it has to do with the uniquely ferocious imagination of Jeter himself. Most sequels attempt a sort of plasticene stretching out of the original text, extruding a narrative here, elongating a familiar character there. Jeter takes the original text, tears it to pieces with his bare teeth, and moulds the resulting mass into striking new shapes. He's not interested in tamely carrying-on Wells's storyline and characters. Instead he takes the book's most iconic items and retools them for the modern age.

In Wells's original story the Morlocks are little more than beasts. That won't do for Jeter's more ornate imaginarium, so he postulates a breed of super-Morlock, cunning, dangerous and capable of large-scale military organisation. Wearing blue spectacles to protect their subterranean eyes from the sun, these blanched-skin horrors have captured the time machine itself and are using it to ferry themselves back to late nineteenth-century London, where they are gathering, in the sewers, with grand and terrible plans.

The book pitches us straight into the storm. One of the things I love about Jeter is his splendidly loose-limbed, unencumbered approach to plotting You never quite know where you are in one of this tales, which, in a genre lamentably oversupplied with predictable narratives, is a very good thing. The novel starts, briskly, just after the end of Wells's novella, but within pages we've been pitched forward into a grisly post-apocalyptic London wasteland, where the remnants of humanity hide like rats in the ruins, and then whisked back again to the nineteenth-century. The more simple-hearted reader, catching their breath at this point, might think that the novel will now follow the straight line of story of resistance to the Morlock invasion leading to a big bang-bang battling climax. But that is not Jeter's way. Instead he makes a series of jolting but brilliant narrative knight's-moves: Merlin, Arthur and Excalibur! Atlantis! A whole subterranean world beneath London, including sunless oceans traversed by Verneian submarines! When some writers throw a whole bunch of disparate elements together the result is a mess: but in Jeter's hands it somehow, madly, coheres.

Picky readers might, I suppose, ask: why does a sequel to Wells's famous time-travel fable also turn out to be an Arthurian novel? It looks on paper (as the phrase goes) like a strange confection, for there is, after all, nothing about King Arthur in Wells's original. This is not to say that it doesn't work, in a weird sort of way; but it is unexpected. I have my own theory about this, although I have no direct evidence for it. I think that Jeter, not wanting to limit himself to textual riffs upon one great nineteenth-century author, played a sort of imaginative textual counterpoint upon another one – Mark Twain, whose *A Connecticut Yankee at King Arthur's Court* (1889) is the other great precursor novel in the traditions of time travel fiction. Although Twain's book came out six years before Wells, its influence on SF has been much less. Some would not even call it science fiction, since it lacks the pseudo-technological for its temporal voyage: there is no machine in Twain's story, his protagonist simply and inexplicably drops back in time to the Arthurian era. But like Wells, the heart of Twain's narrative is really about the plight of the poor under the careless rule of the wealthy, for in Twain's telling, Arthur's knights turn out to be much more cruel and violent than chivalric and noble. I'd be tempted to argue that Wells's approach, by satirically inverting the relationship between aristocracy and proletariate, is more penetrating. But these two core narratives – the one sending a traveller into the far future, the other sending him into the distant past – find a kind of gonzo synthesis in Jeter's Morlock/Arthur mash-up.

The point is that this sort of bravura juxtaposition of elements is exactly right for the kind of novel this is – Steampunk, I mean, a mode of writing that Jeter has a claim to have invented. People sometimes assume that Steampunk is an offshoot of "Cyberpunk", taking the high-tech future-noir adventure of the sort popularised by Bruce Sterling and William Gibson and moving the action back to a steam-powered Babbageized nineteenth-century. In fact Steampunk fiction predates

Cyberpunk (though the name does not). Gibson's *Neuromancer* came out in 1984, and Bruce Bethke's story that gave the movement its moniker, "Cyberpunk", was published in 1983.

But the historians of SF locate the origins of what would later be called Steampunk in three novels by three Californian friends: Jeter's *Morlock Night* (1979), Tim Powers's *The Anubis Gates* (1983) and James P. Blaylock's *Homunculus* (1986). In all three novels, Gothic excess takes the place that is occupied by the conventions of "detective fiction noir" in Cyberpunk itself. And in all three books, London is as much a character as the human players: a gnarly, über-Dickensian city that sprawls both horizontally and exists vertically, from the zeppelins above to the populous sewers below. Indeed, the subterranean locus of much of *Morlock Night* generates a great deal of its dream-haunting power. This is a novel about things that are hidden, that lurk in the collective subconscious: Arthur and Atlantis; Teutonic cruelty and the fear of racial degeneration; the upwelling monstrosity that persists beneath civilisation's thin veneer. It is entirely fitting that the protagonist of the tale discovers that he has never really known who he is.

Steampunk as a mode has, arguably, become diluted with overfamiliarity into a sort of watery tech-y Victoriana. But to read *Morlock Night* is to return to the source. This, ladies and gentlemen, is the real McCoy. Or perhaps I should say, the real MorlocCoy. Jeter's Morlockian night is darker than most, and looks forward to that night that comes to us all eventually. This book is a hectic masterpiece.

Adam Roberts, January 2011

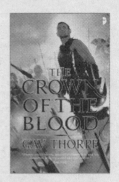

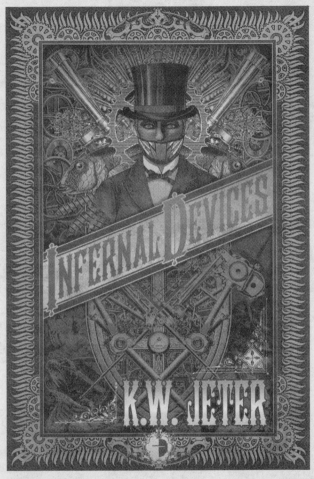

INFERNAL DEVICES

K.W. JETER

"This is the real thing – a mad inventor, curious coins, murky London alleys and windblown Scottish Isles... A wild and extravagant plot that turns up new mysteries with each succeeding page." — *James P Blaylock*